Fried Oyster Sandwich

An Alternative History in the Medium of Fiction

Lloyd E. Gross

authorHOUSE®

AuthorHouse™
1663 Liberty Drive
Bloomington, IN 47403
www.authorhouse.com
Phone: 1 (800) 839-8640

© 2017 Lloyd E. Gross. All rights reserved.

No part of this book may be reproduced, stored in a retrieval system, or transmitted by any means without the written permission of the author.

Published by AuthorHouse 05/08/2017

ISBN: 978-1-5246-8872-1 (sc)
ISBN: 978-1-5246-8871-4 (hc)
ISBN: 978-1-5246-8873-8 (e)

Library of Congress Control Number: 2017906049

Print information available on the last page.

Any people depicted in stock imagery provided by Thinkstock are models, and such images are being used for illustrative purposes only.
Certain stock imagery © Thinkstock.

This book is printed on acid-free paper.

Because of the dynamic nature of the Internet, any web addresses or links contained in this book may have changed since publication and may no longer be valid. The views expressed in this work are solely those of the author and do not necessarily reflect the views of the publisher, and the publisher hereby disclaims any responsibility for them.

Introduction

WELCOME TO NEW ORLEANS IN 1909. This is the largest city and greatest port in the Confederate States of America, forty-four years after its independence was established by the Treaty of Spotsylvania. The capitol is at Richmond. The president is Joseph Draper Sayers of Texas. On her northern border is the United States of America. There is peace between the two republics. Some railroads connect cities in both republics. Soon there will be thirteen Confederate States. Kentucky was awarded to the Confederacy by the treaty, as was the Indian Territory which is soon to become the thirteenth state of Oklahoma. The story of the progress of the War for Southern Independence is told in Appendix A. The subsequent story of how the C.S.A. preserved the Mexican Empire is told in Appendix B. It was necessary to create the subsequent generation of Mexican Hapsburgs. The list of presidents is presented in Appendix C.

It has been twenty-one years since Louisiana abolished slavery, one of the last four states to do so. There was very little conflict about it, and very little disruption. Employment replaced slavery. The law of supply and demand generally determined wages. Confederate money, based on a bi-metallic standard governed by a national bank, is fairly solid. Public morale is very high.

Meet the Kaufmann family. George, the patriarch, was an immigrant from Germany, first to the U.S.A, then to the C.S.A. Eric is his son, now twenty years old. Eric's mother died in the yellow fever epidemic of 1901. He is George's only child. He is a student at Tulane University. He has become involve with Stepahnie Weaver, a student at Sophie Newcombe

College, whose home is in Tulka Oklahoma. Their story is told in Part I. the later parts deal with later generation of Kaufmanns.

Through the eyes of the Kaufmann family, experience this alternative history. They live in it. If you are not familiar with the city, a map would be helpful. If one could be found that wasn't copyrighted, it would probably be here. The story begins in Audubon Park.

Table of Contents

Introduction vii
List of Illustration xi
Part I: The Lost Generation 1
Part II: Henry and Renee 29
Part III: WOPR 77
Part IV: Martin and Lisa 127
Epilogue 193
Appendix A: Southern Independence 197
Appendix B: The Career of the Confederate Expeditionary Force in the Mexican War 219
Appendix C: Presidents of the Confederate States of America 224

List of Illustrations

1. A Garden District House viii
2. A Camp at Milneburg 29
3. A Fried Oyster Sandwich 77
4. A Teletype Machine 95
5. The Café du Monde 127
6. A Pine Tree on the North Shore 166

PART I

The Lost Generation

Chapter One

"This city always smells like a good dinner," said Stephanie as she and Eric walked across Audubon Park on a Friday afternoon. "It's brown sugar and bananas, cloves and thyme, olive oil and garlic. And the French Quarter always smells like malt."

"We have some fine breweries there," Eric replied.

"I'll miss that when I go home for the summer."

"At least you won't be here in the heat."

Stephanie grinned. "Oh, we have our share of that."

It was a Friday afternoon, and Classes were finished for the week. The two young people had headed down to the river and then back to campus across Audubon Park, walking beside a long, narrow lagoon.

"What a perfect day!" cried Stephanie. "It's warm, it's bright, and there's just enough breeze."

"And wonderful company," Eric contributed.

"That boat bobs up and down so softly."

"Look at the squirrels!" cried Eric.

Stephanie looked and saw a mother squirrel leading three young ones along a narrow branch that hung over the lagoon. It was spring in New Orleans.

"As usual, the mother gets stuck with the rearing," she noted.

"Have you ever seen it otherwise?" he asked.

Eric Kaufmann was an only child. His world was an adult world. Stephanie was the oldest, but her twin brothers provided her with more childish folly than her mind could take in. It came as a happy revelation that there were men who were not like her brothers. In the first decade of the twentieth century, men wore ties to school, and often jackets as well. Eric was a man of his times.

Stephanie was his first experience of an Indian, actually a half-Indian, only through her mother. Her long, black hair fell softly behind her. There were no ringlets, which were going out of fashion among women at that time. Her hair hid her ears; it was about four weeks before Eric noticed that she wore earrings. That was so feminine to Eric that he began to find in Stephanie the ideal woman.

Eric was twenty years old in 1909. He was close to completing his junior year at the College of Arts and Sciences at Tulane University. He loved history, was good at writing, and had a good ear for music. His blond hair, hazel eyes, and square face contrasted with Stephanie's swarthy features and black tresses.

Stephanie Weaver was three years younger and was a freshman at Sophie Newcombe College, a women's academy that was part of Tulane University. Saint Charles Avenue separated their campus from Audubon Park. She was Cherokee on her mother's side, but her father was an Easterner from Pennsylvania. He was from mixed English and Ulster Irish families. In spite of the occupational surname, he was a cattle rancher.

As they walked, they passed a live oak tree with roots going everywhere. Stephanie was so focused on the squirrels that she tripped over it, started to roll, and headed for the lagoon. Eric saw what was happening and jumped after her. She kept turning over, but Eric managed to catch her ankle and hang on firmly. Stephanie stopped rolling, although her head was up against a crawfish chimney.

"Now I really feel awkward," Stephanie complained. "I can't believe that happened. And to be rescued by a man!"

"Couldn't you at least say a gentleman?"

"Nothing against you, Eric."

"Did you get your hair wet?"

"Not really, but this muddy thing …"

"The crawfish chimney?"

Stephanie gave a short scream. She had an unusual fear of crustaceans.

"Don't worry," the young man reassured her. "None of them came out. Are you all right otherwise?"

"Give me a minute," she pleaded.

Eric gave her a hand and lifted her until she was standing next to him. The top of her head came to just above his nose. The young woman was not hurt, but she was very embarrassed. Finally, she did manage at a low volume, "Thanks. No injuries. And the memory of this will be a good one overall."

"I'm glad to help you. It isn't about men and women—at least, that's not the first thing here. I would help anyone who fell like that. But you are an attractive woman, which is something I cannot put out of my mind when I'm talking to you. Once that comes into it, nothing can drive it away."

As they resumed their walk, Stephanie replied, "To be fair, then, I should also say that you are a handsome man."

"Then being together is something we like …"

"Until we start on politics."

"And sooner or later, we have to face that. Right?"

"As long as I live, I will be devoted to women's rights."

Eric took Stephanie's hand. "There are so many things that politics addresses. There are trade policies, railroads, currency, foreign relations, industrial organizations …"

"Eric, all of those are important, but can't you see that they affect women as well as men?"

He stopped and turned to face her. "Was that ever in doubt?"

"No, but that makes women's rights all the more important."

Eric thought for a moment and then took Stephanie's hand again and began walking toward the campus. "What about the status of the territory?"

"Do you advocate statehood?"

"I think it makes a lot of sense. But I was wondering if, as an Indian, you might have a different perspective?"

"I have relatives who will never come into mainstream society. To them, it makes no difference whether or not the Territory becomes a state. But my family would like to see statehood."

The wind blew off Eric's straw hat. He chased it over toward the lagoon. Stephanie came after him and caught her breath while he put it back on. "You see, we need the railroads, the agricultural grants, the state university, and a way of fairly distributing the oil revenue."

"Do you write about those things?"

"Not yet," she admitted.

Eric stopped again. "If all of your work is about women, it will make you seem too specialized to be taken seriously. Join it together with statehood."

They arrived at St. Charles Avenue. There were live oak trees giving afternoon shade, their Spanish moss reaching downward. They were more lateral than vertical, and every branch was curved. They sat down under the live oaks. Stephanie asked, "Why do you call these oaks when they don't have oak leaves?"

Eric didn't know. These were the only oak trees he had ever seen. His answer was, "Because they have acorns."

"These acorns look more like olives."

They were brown with yellow heads, and very hard. But to Eric they were acorns. "What can I say?" he said. "This is New Orleans."

That evening Eric was having dinner with his father in the dining room of their white brick house on Second Street, just south of Prytania. An old brick walkway led from the iron gate to the steps that led to a small landing before the front door. George Kaufmann, Eric's father, lived there with him and two servants: Olivia the cook and Essie the maid. They brought the dinner to the two gentlemen of the house and then had their own dinner in the kitchen, where they dined on whatever they liked. George trusted these two women to manage his house. When they left for their dinner, Eric and George were alone at the table. "I had a nice walk across Audubon Park with Stephanie today," Eric began.

"Where did you say she came from?"

"Tulsa," Eric replied, "in the Indian Territory. Her mother is Cherokee, and her father is Irish."

"Like your mother," said George. Eric's mother had died eight years ago in the yellow fever epidemic. "She lived off Magazine Street in the Irish Channel."

"And you are a German immigrant from 1870 who had better things to do than serve in the army," Eric added.

"Her family were immigrants too, before the war. They lived through the occupation, and the chaos that came when the Treaty of Spotsylvania was signed and the Union army left, but no local authority had been established. She was fourteen when I met her in the family's butcher shop on Tchoupitoulas Street."

On the mantelpiece was a picture of Mary Kaufmann. She had dark brown hair and an olive complexion. The next picture showed George in his uniform; he was captain of the Jackson Avenue Ferry. Before that, he had been in the merchant marine, sailing often out of the city. Working for the ferry kept him permanently in New Orleans.

"I remember coming to St. Louis when I first moved to America," said George. "I worked with a grain company at first, and then with some teamsters. But when I saw the river, that changed everything. I saw riverboats flying the Stars and Bars. They told me they were from the South. What they told me sounded better than what I was doing, so I came down here. These coal-burning ferries are my life now."

"From the Garden District to Gretna and back again. Doesn't that get monotonous?"

"It does involve repetition," George answered, "but there are always different ships and boats about on the river."

"I'll have to take Stephanie for a ferry ride."

"Why don't you bring her here? I'd like to meet her."

Olivia came in and asked, "Are you gentlemen ready for dessert?"

"That would be great," Eric replied.

"Were you answering me or Olivia?" George asked.

"Oh. Olivia," Eric answered. "But I'm sure Stephanie would be able to come here. I'm both local and a student, so the university's rules would permit me to bring her here."

"She isn't going to talk about Cubism, is she?" That art form was very popular, but George had no use for it.

"Don't be surprised if she talks about women in politics," said Eric.

Olivia brought in a bread pudding, which she covered with rum. She dished it out to George and Eric. Then Essie brought in coffee, which Olivia mixed with a small amount of cognac. George and Eric stopped talking and dug into the food.

The following week on Saturday, after a picnic lunch in Audubon Park, Eric and Stephanie crossed over the levee to walk on the batture. A short way from the park, there was a bench on the batture, where they sat down to talk. Looking at the river was stimulating for both of them.

"This comes all the way from Minnesota," was Stephanie's way of beginning. "I've never seen the northern part of it."

"Where else have you seen it?"

"St. Louis."

"Really? That's where my father used to live."

"My parents took me there when I was about eleven. I remember the riverboats. There were always more of them there than anywhere else."

Eric sat very close to Stephanie. He found her very interesting. "Do you like New Orleans enough to want to stay here?" he asked.

"Do you mean, would I rather go back to the ranch?" she asked.

"Would you?"

"I have two brothers," she said. "They're twins, about fourteen years old now. They have red hair like my father. They used to play mean tricks on me. Sammy and Danny are more than enough to take care of the ranch."

"Did your father arrange a marriage for you?"

"Like the New Orleans girls? Nobody in Oklahoma does that. We don't come out when we're seventeen. And I don't think the New Orleans girls like the way they're put on display."

"I really never discussed the matter with them. But I know the men are very independent about it. They don't like being told whom to marry."

"Your father doesn't expect you to marry his choice?"

"He isn't high society. And personally, I think the debutantes are too young. College is the place to find a good woman."

"I was seventeen when I enrolled here," Stephanie replied.

A large steamship came pushing its way upstream. "Let's go up on the levee," said Eric. "That wake is going to splash the batture."

"I'll put the picnic cloth on the ground."

"That should work. I think Missouri wishes it were part of our country instead of the United States. It's an agricultural state with few large urban areas."

"From what I've seen of both countries, they aren't all that different. Do they think their allegiance would make a difference?"

"It was divided during the war. Troops from Illinois came over and subdued it. But the Germans were nearly all on the side of the Union."

"Why was that?"

"The large number of Forty-Eighters. They were socialist agitators who left Europe after they were defeated in 1848. It's true that the Saxons came earlier, for religious reasons. But it only took about ten years, and then they were the minority of Germans."

"Tell me about the religion."

"The Saxons?"

"Yes."

"They were true Lutherans. When their king died, the Land of Saxony came into the kingdom of Prussia. The Prussian king wanted only one church in his realm, so he told the Lutherans and the Reformed to merge, say the same prayers, sing the same hymns, and share the Holy Eucharist—even though the Reformed do not believe in the Real Presence."

There was a small amount of fruit juice left in the bottle they had brought. Stephanie took a drink and then asked, "What's the Real Presence?"

Eric also took a drink and replied, "That Jesus gives us His very Body and Blood in the Holy Eucharist. That teaching goes back to the origins of Christianity, but the Reformed claim that the elements merely represent the Lord."

"I've never heard about anyone fighting about such a thing."

"It's been a long time since any blood was shed, but the verbal confrontations continue to this day."

"Did all the Lutherans believe this?"

"Many thought it was not a critical teaching, and so they went along with the merging. But Bishop Stefan's group emigrated rather than merge. They first landed here, and then they chartered four steamboats. Most of them went on to Missouri."

"And the others?"

"They're still here in New Orleans. They have a couple of downtown churches, as well as Zion, which I showed you from the streetcar."

"Maybe we should start back," Stephanie suggested. Eric helped her fold the picnic blanket, and they started down the levee, back into the park. She asked, "Why did your father leave Missouri?"

"Economic opportunity. He met my mother when he used to live by the Irish Channel. She was Irish, and her father had a butcher shop there. But she died in the epidemic of 1901. My Grandpa O'Brien lives on Magazine Street now. He's very old and hardly ever goes out these days."

"Your family is nearly all men. No wonder you're so patriarchal!"

"My mother read Jane Austen books to me."

"Nice dodge. You don't want to talk about politics."

He smiled. "Talk? Of course I'll talk about politics. I just don't want to argue about them."

"I see your point. So think about the Court House on Royal Street. Think about the legend over the front door …"

"This is a government of laws, not of men."

She said, "Right. Does that mean a government of laws is a government of women?

"Hardly. But no one ever has a government of laws."

"Then why do they call it that?"

"To deceive us. We have a government of men."

"Are the men above the law?"

"Have you ever heard of legislators?" he countered.

"Yes, of course."

"They have authority to change the law. So we really have a government of legislators. They can even amend the Constitution. If you really wanted a government of laws, those laws would have to be unchangeable. As it is, the law is simply a weapon the men hold, by which they govern." He tossed his straw hat in the air, but Stephanie intercepted it. She began to run toward the university. When they came to the live oaks, she had to slow down, and Eric overtook her. She threw the hat behind him. When he retrieved it, she came back to hug him.

Eric invited Stephanie to dinner at the German restaurant on St. Charles Avenue. As they passed by Zion Church on the streetcar, he pointed out that he had been confirmed there. He was at ease navigating the menu and explaining the offerings to his date. They enjoyed a local beer.

"Did you go to church in Tulsa?" he asked.

"No," she replied. "My father did pray at home. My mother read the Bible to me, but not very often."

"So you were never confirmed?"

"No. Neither were Sammy or Danny."

"Did your family ever have slaves?"

"No, but the Cherokee nation did. They were the last to emancipate them."

"Olivia had been a slave once," he said. "She worked for a free Negro master who owned a shrimp boat at Shell Beach on Lake Borgne. In 1888, Louisiana freed the slaves. She continued to work for him until he died, and then she came to New Orleans. She cooked for families, so my father hired her to cook the seafood she had known all her life."

"What did you say this was?" she asked.

"Wiener schnitzel. That means a chop from Vienna. We also have Essie working for us. She was born before 1888 but was too young to remember slavery. Her mother worked for a Creole family in the French Quarter. She's Catholic."

"And you've always been Lutheran?"

"When I was in school, my teacher asked me what denomination I was. I knew Dad was Lutheran, so I said that was what I was. He took me to Zion Church at Easter. When we got home, he showed me my baptismal certificate. It was from an Episcopal Church. But Pastor Clausner told me what confirmation was. So I learned the catechism."

"What about your mother? What did she think?"

"She died when I was twelve, in the yellow fever epidemic. She's buried in the cemetery on Washington Avenue, not far from our house."

After dinner, they went back to the streetcar. As they went around Lee Circle, Eric pointed out that the tracks were now on the neutral ground.

"Neutral ground?"

"I guess that term is strange to you. Back before the war, the English settlers who live in the Garden District migrated here from Virginia. They were 'uptown.' The Creoles who lived on the other side of Canal Street were 'downtown.' Often there was friction between their young men. Each stayed on his own side of Canal Street, but the median in the middle of Canal Street was available to both groups. Thus it became known as neutral ground. Ever since then, any median in a New Orleans street is known by that name."

Soon they passed by Second Street. Eric pointed it out and invited Stephanie to meet his father. They made an appointment, which George approved when Eric got home that night. Eric was entertaining the notion of marrying Stephanie, but he had no idea of the details yet.

He wanted to wait until she finished her course of study at Newcombe. The question of whether they loved one another was one he could not answer; he had never asked Stephanie whether or not she loved him. He asked George for advice and was told it was best to be frank about the matter.

Eric invited Stephanie to his house, to have dinner in the large dining room. Stephanie could smell Olivia's cooking as soon as Essie opened the front door.

"You have a banana tree in your yard," she pointed out to Eric.

"One in front and one in back. And yes, we do get fruit from them every year."

"It smells so good here. Is Olivia making dinner?"

"Yes, and she's doing extra because of this special occasion."

George entered as Eric was speaking, and Eric introduced him to Stephanie. She had put her hair in braids, so in spite of wearing her best dress, she looked especially Indian that evening. George had acquired excellent manners while living in the Garden District, and he charmed his son's girlfriend from the beginning. Eric offered her a glass of Sherry. She looked at the high ceiling, which was about a foot higher than most American houses, though it was very typical of New Orleans at the time, even in the working-class neighborhoods. With the temperature seldom falling below forty degrees, heating these rooms was not a difficult problem.

They sat in a living room with well-upholstered chairs facing an equally well-upholstered sofa around a fairly large space. Across from the sofa was a fireplace framed neatly by a mantelpiece. On top of the mantelpiece was a shelf with a ticking clock, which was mock Hepplewhite. George and Eric did not have pets, but there were a number of foliage houseplants. Directly in front of the sofa was a coffee table, on top of which a lacquered pewter bowl sat on a small doily. This afternoon the bowl was filled with green grapes.

Eric and Stephanie sat on the sofa. George poured himself a glass of Sherry and then brought the bowl of grapes to Stephanie. "Have some, Stephanie."

"Thanks."

"You, too, Eric."

"Thanks, Dad. Stephanie and I are so fortunate to live where there are such good universities. The United States has those land grant schools. But we do very well with universities like Duke, Vanderbilt, and William and Mary."

George replied, "And our local schools are excellent. We have the endowment of Paul Tulane and the Catholic Loyola University of the South."

"Eric pointed that out to me when we were walking through Audubon Park. Its bell tower is so striking," said Stephanie.

George asked Stephanie about her family. She talked about her brothers and her parents. Then Essie came in to call them to the dining room.

At dinner, the conversation turned to the threat of European war. The Confederacy was loyal to France for historical reasons, but it was also concerned to be allied with the United States. Sides were being formed. Italy and Turkey had joined the Central Powers, and Russia was part of the Entente with Britain and France. Spain, the Netherlands, and Sweden were neutral and unwilling to change that status. Egypt was a colony of Britain, as was Malta. Tunisia, Algeria, and Morocco were colonies of France. Syria, Palestine, and Lebanon belonged to the Ottomans. Lybia was an Italian colony.

George was the first to express an opinion. "Without Bismarck, Germany has no leader who can keep it out of war. She wants to build the Berlin to Baghdad railroad, and so far she has a clear road through Budapest. After that, she has treaties that take the course from Sofia to Antioch. Where she needs to develop is the Balkans."

Stephanie showed her geographical acumen when she asked, "With Britain and France primarily sea powers, don't the Germans and Austrians have to develop trade over land?"

"They could try to develop a trade zone with Russia and Sweden that would depend on the Baltic Sea," Eric contributed. "But primarily they have to look southeast. I have no idea how Italy fits into this."

Stephanie noted, "Italy has support in the Adriatic from Austria, and further east from Turkey."

"That's not enough," said George. "Britain has Egypt and Malta."

Olivia cleared the soup dishes and brought out the salad, which today was hearts of palm.

"And where do the Yanks come in?" asked Eric.

"They're divided," said George, "but they're surrounded on every side by countries that are either British or allied with France."

"Do you think the Germans could pry Mexico away from France?" asked Stephanie. She knew the story of the Confederate Expeditionary Force and the role her own people had played in the war against Juarez.

Eric knew that since their horrible defeat in 1870, the French did not really care much about Mexico. However, he did not want to embarrass Stephanie.

George had a suggestion. "If the hostility spreads to South America, Chile and Argentina could side with the Central Powers. Uruguay might be hard to predict, but the other states would be neutral."

"And the Canal?" asked Eric.

"Isn't that the Yanks' problem?" George quipped. "Mexico doesn't have a navy, and we don't have a Pacific Coast. If the Yanks stay neutral, the Canal stays open."

"I might suggest one more scenario," continued Stephanie. "We become allies with the United States. Then we could both be neutral."

"Like Spain?" asked Eric.

"And every country in South America that doesn't have a large German population," George replied.

"Can we put Fort Sumpter behind us forever?" Stephanie asked.

"The Treaty of Spotsylvania solved that," said Eric.

Essie came in again to pour the dinner wine. When she finished. Olivia entered in with a bowl of pasta and a platter of *daube creole*. There was a lull in the conversation as all three enjoyed the main course.

When dinner came to an end, the three returned to the salon for coffee and Cognac. George wanted a cigar, and so the young people went out to the front porch, where Eric immediately turned the conversation to personal matters.

"Do you have any idea how attracted I am to you, Stephanie?"

"Of course. I am a girl, you know."

"That's a good beginning. But I see this as something far greater. When I think of what I will be doing twenty years from now, I see myself with you."

"I can't say I ever looked that far ahead, but having you around would be nice," she admitted.

"So I'm asking you to marry me, Stephanie."

"I was hoping you would."

"Because you wanted to answer yes?"

"Yes, Eric. I want to marry you. Is that clear enough?"

"It couldn't be clearer. We need to make plans."

Chapter Two

Eric was reading the paper as he sat in the kitchen of his house on Clermont Drive in Edgewood. He and Stephanie had moved there as soon as they had enough money to buy it. It was 1916, and Eric was working for the *Times-Picayune*, a recent merger of two daily morning papers. He wrote historical feature stories and local social events. They had been married in the summer of 1911 in Tulsa. Then they moved in with George until they'd bought this house. It was a small house, but Stephanie loved it. It had a high gable over the front door and was wider than it was deep. It sat near the front of the lot, but there was room for a front yard with an evergreen. There was a larger backyard with a pecan tree. Stephanie had a garden in the back, against the house, and she grew flowers from April to October. Their son, Henry, had just turned three in January. Stephanie was pregnant again, and she was fully occupied as a wife and mother. George still steamed across the river every day on the Jackson Avenue Ferry.

Stephanie became a Lutheran, and they had Henry baptized at Zion Church near George's house while they were living there. They joined a church on Burgundy Street between the river and St. Claude Avenue. They did not own an automobile, but the Gentilly streetcar passed two blocks east along Franklin Avenue, and they could ride to church with their neighbors, the Bauers.

The news in Eric's paper was about the war in Europe. Of the North American powers, both republics had remained neutral. Canada, of course, was British. The United States had its share of unrest. The New York–New England coalition of industries, banks, and commercial interests was facing opposition from the Midwest, where a wave of populism had developed in the 1890s. The population of the Midwest was mainly German and Irish, neither of whom thought much of England. Another railroad had been finished, joining New Orleans with Cincinnati through Nashville and Louisville.

Stephanie's marching suffragettes were receiving less attention. In the United States, there was a call for a constitutional amendment to allow woman suffrage. Eric sighed because he saw nothing about the topic that concerned him chiefly—namely, the levees. He would do something about that.

The previous summer, New Orleans had been hit by a rather strong hurricane. Eric and Stephanie were still living with George in the Garden District, a low-lying area, and so they witnessed some of the flooding, but it did not get inside the house. Stephanie was awestruck by the event. She was used to tornados in Tulsa, which were frightening but of much shorter duration. She tried to stay busy with little Henry, but the winds were distracting. Doctors and nurses stayed at the hospitals until the storm was over. Everyone else stayed home. In the early afternoon, the wind damaged the roof. Eric asked Olivia and Essie to look after Henry. He held Stephanie on his lap on a large chair in the living room, and he talked softly to her until the wind died down, which it did around dinnertime. The rain lasted all through the night, but that was the extent of it.

Eric was a feature writer, but he knew a thing or two about investigative work. Soon after the hurricane, he started research for a series of articles about the geographical situation of the city. At first, the response was denial, but Eric was very convincing. One day as he sat at his desk, he received a telephone call from the mayor. The city was appointing a committee to make recommendations about the city's preparedness to deal with hurricanes, and he wanted Eric to chair that committee.

As soon as the mayor was off the phone, Eric called Stephanie. He told her about the appointment and asked her opinion as to whether or not he should accept it. Stephanie knew what had just happened. There was still something of the suffragette inside of her that took some offense in the fact that a group of men was being appointed. She repressed the thought quickly, but she could not give Eric an opinion. They would discuss it at supper.

While riding home on the streetcar, Eric had a good look at St. Charles Avenue. Many houses had roof damage. City crews were still clearing the side streets, where trees had been blown over. He walked up the walkway, up the steps, and to the front door. Essie opened the door for him and accompanied him to the dining room, where Stephanie was waiting. "How was your day?" she asked.

"All I could think about was the committee," he answered. "How are things here?"

"Henry was a good boy. Your father isn't home yet from the ferry. I think Olivia has dinner ready."

Essie left for the kitchen as Eric put his jacket away and then came to the table and sat down. He looked straight at Stephanie.

"So should I take it?" asked Eric.

"Does it pay anything?"

"Only expenses. We have lunch meetings and have to get there on our own."

She asked, "Does the paper know you're going to be away all those days at lunchtime?"

"I told Warren about the proposal. He did not seem too concerned."

Olivia came in and asked, "Should I serve the soup, Mister Kaufmann?"

"My father isn't home yet, Olivia. Is it important to serve it now?"

"No, sir. It will stay warm in the pot."

"Then let's give him a little longer," said Stephanie.

"That'll be fine, Mrs. Kaufmann," said Olivia.

Stephanie got back to the discussion. "Is it worth the extra time?"

"Good question. I have to answer it on two levels. On the family level, it won't make much difference. But on the civic level, it could be the most important work being done in New Orleans."

"So are you the man for the job?"

"The mayor called me because of my articles. The same sources I read are at the library for anyone who wants to read them. But because I have already done that, it would save a few steps."

They heard George approaching the front door, and Essie went to let him in. Eric got up to welcome his father as Essie took his jacket and cap. They waited for George as he went to greet his grandson. When he came and sat at the table, Olivia brought the soup.

"We've been discussing an offer the mayor made to Eric," said Stephanie.

"Really? What was that?" George asked.

Eric said, "He wants me to head a committee to discuss how New Orleans is prepared for hurricanes."

"I read your articles," said Stephanie. "Is the situation really that serious?"

"Can't you see that?" Eric countered.

George answered him. "New Orleans has been here since 1718—one hundred ninety-eight years. So far it has survived."

"Before that, who knows how many times it was inundated?" said Eric.

"There were no levees then," George replied.

"Of course not, but that doesn't mean …"

Olivia cleared the soup bowls and brought in a platter of fried chicken. Essie brought in a large bowl of salad. George filled the glasses with Chablis. Stephanie picked up a baguette, broke it, and handed her husband a slice.

After he munched his slice, Eric continued. "That doesn't mean the levees would have held."

Stephanie had questions of her own. "What about the lake?" she asked.

"Water from the lake would come up the New Basin Canal," Eric answered. "It could get as far as City Park Avenue. We have pumping stations now on Orleans Avenue, and we're building one on London Avenue. We have none on the bayou or the New Basin. And consider east of the bayou. What defenses have Milneburg or Little Woods?"

"The committee would consider all that?" asked George.

"I would insist on it."

"Then, Eric, you should be on it," said Stephanie. "Make our children proud."

The next day, Eric approached the desk of Warren Salvatore, the city editor to whom he reported. "I've decided to accept the appointment. Are you sure the paper will be all right with this?"

"All right?" the editor replied. "That means we will be on that committee. You can keep us up to date on everything it does. Believe me, the readers will want to know this."

"I don't want to scare the general public."

"Yes, you do. At least, you want them to take the hurricane flood situation seriously. And they are not likely to do that without at least a small hint of a threat."

Eric nodded. "Give me a little time after each meeting to sift the ideas that come up before I write about them."

"Are our competitors involved on the committee?"

"No."

"Then a day of two won't matter. It will give you more time to compose the articles."

"Would you like a few editorials as well?"

"Do a trial one, and we'll go from there," Warren said.

"Thanks. It looks as if we're in agreement. The committee will have to recommend specific action. The conflict will come over how much it costs."

"You wanted a political appointment, Eric. That goes with the territory."

Chapter Three

For Thanksgiving 1916, the family met for dinner at George's house. Olivia had prepared a fine feast. Linda, the newest Kaufmann, had been born in August, shortly after Eric's committee met for the first time. She had been baptized at Zion Church near George's house, but the church Eric and Stephanie joined was the one on Burgundy Street. Stephanie's brother, Danny, had come down to be Linda's godfather.

"I'm so glad to have my grandchildren here," said George. "I bought a car so I could visit them when they can't make it here."

"I didn't think it was to go to work," said Stephanie. The ferry was in walking distance.

"We're getting a new boat soon," said George. "It's being built in Algiers."

"You're replacing that old one, aren't you, Dad?"

"More than just that. We're going to have side ramps to carry automobiles across the river. It still has the large common room and the promenade deck."

"Is it expensive?" asked Stephanie.

"Because of the war, some things are going to be."

Fried Oyster Sandwich

"We kept out of the war," said Eric. "I'm glad we did. The European nations are drafting young men for their armies. They have revived the Bonapartist idea of the *levee en masse*. If we got involved in that mess, I might get called up."

Course after course kept coming from the kitchen, and it was finally completed with a mincemeat pie. As in previous years, Essie brought out the coffee while Olivia poured a little cognac in each cup.

"Dad," Stephanie began, "Henry asked me what a ferry captain did. What shall I tell him?"

"Quite a bit," George began. "He rides the ferries back and forth, delays their departure on foggy days, observes and evaluates the pilots, reviews the purchases of fuel and other necessities, hires and supervises the employees (whether sailors, stevedores, or officers), and does his best to improve the public image of his line."

"I doubt Henry could grasp all that," she replied. "Could I find a simple answer?"

"Let's try this: he tells the ferry people what to do."

"That's perfect," said Stephanie with a smile.

Eric was reading the paper. There was no sign that the war in Europe was heading for a resolution. The Germans and Austrians had had a successful offensive in Poland the year before, but the Western Front was a stalemate that now included casualty lists unheard of before. He knew the French were courting the Confederate States as an ally, but he also knew there was no advantage to be gained by becoming belligerent. The British were engaged in a campaign to chase the Turks out of the Middle East. On the next page, he read that New Orleans was still the busiest port in the country, with Norfolk and Jacksonville closely behind. that Houston had decided to build a ship channel to bring blue water vessels right into the city. He looked in vain for news about his levee project. An editorial suggested that the war was good for business. He started thinking about his next feature, advocating construction of a spillway to divert floodwater from the Mississippi into Lake Pontchartrain. He stood alone in not letting the matter rest. Before he could address it again, though, he had a promise to keep: a feature about the camps at Milneburg and access to them.

At the age of twenty-seven, Eric was a journalistic prodigy. The year 1917 was when Warren Salvatore was promoted to editorial page editor. One of his first moves was to request Eric as his chief editorial writer. There was a salary increase, which helped now that the baby was growing so quickly. Henry was four years old, and Eric bought him some new clothes and a new pair of shoes. He took his son for a long ride on the street car, transferring twice and shopping in a part of town that was new to the little boy but somewhat familiar to Eric, because it was near his father's house. There was money for a new outfit for Linda, which everybody knew she would outgrow in a few months. As for Stephanie, there was a new table in the kitchen with chairs to match. However, after the initial spending, the family settled down to a realistic budget, which served them very well.

The war took an unexpected turn that year. There was a thorough revolution in Russia. The tsar and his family were imprisoned. The Bolsheviks made peace with Germany and Austria, so there was no more Eastern Front. Eric again tried to convince his committee that the spillway was a workable solution. The rest of the committee thought it was too ambitious, so they tabled it indefinitely. It would be ten years before he could resurrect it, due to severe spring floods that year. By that time, Eric was no longer writing features. He was editor of the editorial page and was no longer on the committee. However, he did get another raise. With their new resources, he and Stephanie were able to buy a camp in Milneburg to spend their summer vacations on Lake Pontchartrain.

Part II

Henry and Renee

Chapter Four

The train ran down the middle of Elysian Fields Avenue, taking the weekend and summer vacationers to Milneburg. With the coming of the automobile, the tracks beyond Florida Avenue were removed. Blacktopped roads led the travelers to Lake Pontchartrain. They could go westward along the shore to West End, at the end of the New Basin Canal. However, most of the travelers went eastward, to the Milneburg camps.

Once one crossed the Industrial Canal heading east, one came to a long line of these camps, wooden one-story houses built on wooden stilts slightly away from the shore, accessed by wooden walkways on stilts, most of which had gates. The Southern Railway, having left Elysian Fields and headed east, crossed the Industrial Canal by a drawbridge, which had one lane each way on its sides for the auto road to use. Every afternoon at 4:00, the *Rebel* came by on its way to Mobile and Jacksonville. It was the crack train of the Gulf, Mobile, and Ohio Railroad. This was the eastbound *Rebel*, which followed the Southern Railway tracks until those split off to go to Slidell and eventually Lynchburg, Virginia. Then it followed the Louisville and Nashville tracks until those went northward to Montgomery, Birmingham, and the cities for which it was named. After that, it followed its own rails to Pensacola and on to the east coast.

Henry Kaufmann came by every summer afternoon while his family was vacationing in its lakeside camp. He was familiar with the railroad—its turns, rises, falls, as well as the schedule of all the trains of the three railroads that used it. This was one of two eastern exits from New Orleans. Henry's camp was about a mile and a half east of the canal bridge. Trains going east would always sound their whistles when they crossed the bridge, so he was well aware when they were coming. Westbound trains were not so well announced, but they came mostly in the morning or after 6:00 p.m.

On a Thursday afternoon in June 1926, Henry was walking across the causeway to his camp toward the road and the railroad beyond it. How different this area was from the Garden District, where his grandfather lived! The record player in his parents' camp was rather loud. Even at the far side of a seventy-foot causeway, he could still hear it playing a jazzy tune. He walked in rhythm with the music he was hearing. The brackish smell of Lake Pontchartrain was in the air, but there was no hint of rain.

A person caught his attention. Thirteen-year-old Henry saw a girl walking along the Gulf, Mobile, and Ohio tracks. She was smaller than he was, and she was too far away for him to tell whether or not he knew her. The Petersons, who had the camp just east of his, had a daughter, Dorothy, who was a year younger than he—but this girl was not Dorothy. She was about three camps from his, walking eastward and approaching his camp slowly. Henry considered the time of day and realized there was a problem. The tracks at this point were on a man-made foundation, with swamp on both sides. The *Rebel* would be coming soon, and the only place to get out of its way was into the swamp. There were snakes in the swamp and various other life forms, including crustaceans and a few large rodents. Henry thought he should warn her, because it was near time for the *Rebel* to pass.

Henry quickened his pace. The girl kept coming. He shouted at her, but she couldn't understand him. Finally he walked quickly up to her. "The *Rebel* is coming soon," he said loudly. "We have to get off the tracks before it gets here."

The girl stopped. "Is the train coming? Is that what you're telling me?" she asked.

Fried Oyster Sandwich

Henry walked westward toward the approaching streamliner and stopped face to face with the girl. "This is risky business now," he said.

"But there's no place to go but the swamp," the girl replied.

"I'm sorry about that. We can walk toward my camp. Please, follow me now." They heard the whistle as the train approached the bridge. Henry knew he had two minutes, no more. They might not make it to his camp, but if they had to go into the swamp, it would be as close to his camp as possible. When the girl heard the whistle, she started to run, tripped over a railroad tie, and fell down onto the tracks. Henry picked her up and carried her toward his camp. He was surprised at how light the girl was. He knew better than to run and so walked very deliberately. The girl held onto his neck tightly. He thought she was afraid.

"I see the locomotive!" she cried.

They were still one camp from Henry's, but he didn't want to wait on the tracks any longer. "Here's where we get off," he said. He walked down into the swamp and put down the girl. There was a strong wind as the train went by, but they were safe. "We can go back on the tracks now," he said. The danger was past, and they were only wet to the knee. As they climbed back onto the tracks, the girl saw she had lost a shoe in the swamp. She was still somewhat panicky, and so she froze. Henry led her as well as he could. She appeared to be hurt.

"I have something in my foot," she said.

"As light as you are, that's not a problem," said Henry as he carried her again. When they arrived at the porch of his camp, she was still clinging to him fiercely. "I'm Henry Kaufmann. This is my parents' camp."

"My name is Renee," she said. "I can't believe that just happened." She was twelve years old but was small for her age. Henry had thought she was younger.

"You can let go now," he said, seating her in a chair on the porch. "Are you staying at one of the camps here, Renee?"

"Yes," she said, "with the Petersons. Gingerbread."

"That's the next camp east. My parents are Eric and Stephanie Kaufmann. We live in New Orleans. This camp is called Tulsa." The camps along Lake Pontchartrain had names. Some were casual names, like Breezewood or Frank's Folly. Some were nostalgic, like Memory Land or Dreamboat. The one where Renee's neighbors were staying was called Gingerbread. But Stephanie wanted to think about her hometown, so she and Eric called theirs Tulsa.

"I'm Renee Gautier," the girl replied. "I live in New Orleans too, on North Claiborne Avenue near Desire Street. But we used to live in New Iberia. We're Acadiens." By this, she meant her ancestors had been deported from Nova Scotia in the mid-eighteenth century and had settled in what was then a Spanish colony in Louisiana, west of the Mississippi. "We moved here six years ago so my father could work on the Watson and Williams Bridge. He's a surveyor."

The bridge of which she spoke was a few miles east of Milneburg, where a peninsula called Pointe aux Herbes projected about a mile into the east basin of the lake. A highway from New Orleans was destined to cross the lake over that bridge.

Stephanie came out onto the porch, surprised to see her son talking to a girl.

"Hi, Mom," said Henry. "This is Renee. I met her a few minutes ago."

"I was walking down the tracks. I didn't know the *Rebel* was coming, but Henry did. He went out there to rescue me."

"Goodness!" replied Stephanie. "How old are you, Renee?"

"I was twelve last May," she said. "I fell down. Henry had to carry me to a safe place."

The two youths were attracted to each other but were only beginning to become aware of it. Stephanie could see it, and she expected they would both be awkward about it. "I made some lemonade," she said. "You could both use a glass of it. Linda?" Henry's sister appeared. "Would you please bring us two glasses?"

"Who's that girl?" Linda asked.

"Her name is Renee," Henry answered, and then he added, "Excuse me for a minute." He walked to the bathroom.

"The glasses please, Linda," said Stephanie.

"Okay, but I want to know what's going on," said Linda.

"I'm Renee Gautier, Mrs. Kaufmann," said the girl. "I live in New Orleans on North Claiborne. Right now we're staying with the Petersons at Gingerbread."

"You must be a friend of Dorothy's," said Stephanie.

"We live next door to her."

"So your parents are out here too?"

"Yes. Our neighbors invited us. Dorothy and I are good friends."

Just then, Henry returned. He was wearing khaki shorts and a white T-shirt with dry brown socks. He was carrying a bath towel. "Renee, you probably would like dry feet too."

She hadn't noticed that her legs were wet from the swamp, but she was aware now.

"What happened to your shoe?" asked Stephanie as Linda put the glasses on the coffee table.

"I think I lost it in the swamp," Renee answered.

"We didn't have time to get to the shelled area. The *Rebel* was coming. We had to get off the tracks where we were." Henry sat on the floor at Renee's feet. "Just relax," he said, "I know you're still tense."

He had a chance to look Renee over carefully. She was wearing a knee-length blue dress with a white shirt underneath. She had white anklet socks and one maroon loafer, which Henry was in the process of removing. She had no rings or bracelets, but wore a pewter neck chain with a cross. Her dark brown hair was cut close to her face; one could probably picture her with a cloche hat. She carried no bag of any kind, but she had a small handkerchief in her pocket, which she offered to Henry. "This towel is more than enough," he said. As Stephanie and Linda went into the living room so the mother could tell her daughter what was going on, Henry stripped off Renee's wet sock and dried her foot. "I'm thirteen since January," he said. He focused on the foot he was drying. "You have small feet," he said. "Are you sure you're twelve?"

"Definitely. As of last May. You're very kind, Henry."

He stopped. "Now for your other foot," he said.

"That's the hurt foot."

"Where did you hurt it?"

"After I got back on the tracks without a shoe."

Henry liked spending time with Renee. "I'll be very careful drying this one." As he dried it, he examined is as best he could. "What's this?" he asked as he found a small piece of gravel that had worked its way into the ridge at the base of her toes.

"What do you think it is? I hope it's not a creature from the swamp."

"No, this is from the rail bed," he said. "I can get it." He pulled out a pocket knife and folded out the metal nail file that was attached to it. Renee had not moved.

Stephanie came back in. "Does she have a splinter, Henry?"

"No, it's a little rock from the rail bed, lodged in one of the lines on her foot. I can get it out, Mom."

Henry was focused on Renee. Not only was she with him, but he was taking care of her. He had not expected to spend the afternoon this way, but now that it was happening, he didn't want it to end. As he uncurled her toes and started to extract the little pebble, Renee giggled. She knew he wasn't trying to annoy her. "Do you like girls?" she asked.

"I don't really know many girls at school. I like Linda, and I definitely like you."

"How did that little thing get inside my sock?"

"Through a hole."

"It didn't have a hole when I put it on."

"It has two now that you've been walking on the tracks without a shoe. You must have put your full weight on it. The pebble didn't cut you, but it lodged itself in that little line. That's why it hurt."

Again he tried to dislodge the pebble, but Renee started wiggling and giggling. He tightened his grip on her foot. "Do you like me in spite of the fact that I'm a girl?" she asked.

Henry had no idea how to answer that. He hadn't been thinking anything like that. "Why do you ask?"

"We girls are more ticklish than boys. Is that annoying you?"

"No," Henry insisted. "I think I like you more because you're a girl." He thought about what he had just said as he made another attempt with the file. As Renee giggled, he assured her, "There's something exciting about taking care of a girl like you." Finally the little pebble was dislodged, and he dropped it on the floor.

"Thank you. Do you want to kiss it to make it better?" she asked.

"Whatever makes you think that would work?" he asked.

"My mother always said it did."

Stephanie intervened. "I never did that with Henry, but I know a lot of parents who do."

"Can I just rub it instead?" Henry asked.

"You can rub it all you like," Renee replied.

Stephanie picked up Renee's socks to hang them outside. "They'll be dry in an hour. Would you like to borrow a pair of Linda's sandals so you can walk home?"

Henry turned to his mother, "Does she have to go, Mom?"

"Do you think her parents are worried about her?"

"Not yet," said Renee.

"Well, I'll get the sandals anyway," Stephanie said as she went back into the camp.

Henry was still rubbing Renee's foot. "As far as I'm concerned, you can stay barefoot as long as you stay here." She was alive and warm; her skin was soft and smooth.

"Wait till I tell Dorothy about this," she said. "Are you really sure kissing it wouldn't help?" Renee didn't get the area of the brain that boys associated with kissing. Henry didn't know how to tell her about it because he had never put it into words before. He stopped rubbing. "You saved my life, Henry. I owe you everything."

Now he was embarrassed. Reason convinced him that Renee was right, but his heart couldn't quite grasp the importance of it. He started to get up, but Renee said, "Please don't put my foot down yet. It feels much better, and your fingers are so gentle." She curled her toes into his palm. There wasn't a trace of nail polish on them.

Stephanie entered again with the sandals.

"Just put them down here, Mom," said Henry. "She doesn't need them yet." He looked up at Renee's eyes and realized she was very happy.

"She's very grateful to you, Henry," said Stephanie. "You're her hero today. And you're a lucky boy, to be a hero for such a lovely girl."

"I think Henry's happy with me too," said Renee. "I can't imagine anything better happening. I really don't need to go yet."

"Do you want to stay for supper?" asked Henry.

"No, my parents and the Petersons would want me before that." Henry put Renee's foot down. "Why are you putting it down?" she asked.

"The sandals," he answered. "Let's see how they fit you." It didn't take long to find out that they were a bit too big. "These are my little sister's," said Henry, "and she's only ten!"

"I only have to wear them to the next camp," said Renee. "I think I can keep them on that long."

"I want to see you soon."

"I want you to meet my parents, and Dorothy," said Renee. "They need to see my hero."

"We'll be looking forward to seeing you later," said Stephanie. Then she went inside. Renee stood up next to Henry.

"I'm glad I met you," said Henry. "You're the nicest girl I know."

"Now you keep still," said Renee. She put her lips to his cheek and gave him a little circle of five kisses. He was glad Linda didn't see that. He fumbled for a minute about how to respond, and then he put his arm around her shoulders and gave her a hug. When they were face to face again, Renee said, *Merci, mon ami.* He had never heard a parting word spoken so softly.

As they were having supper, Linda saw people coming up the walkway. Eric looked and saw Renee and two adults, apparently her parents. They wanted to meet Henry. Stephanie got up and then went to the door with Henry and Linda. Maurice and Jackie were impressed with Henry, and they spent a few minutes fussing over him while Linda talked to Renee. Stephanie was glad to see Renee again, and she commented on how pretty she was. Finally, Maurice greeted Eric and thanked him for having Henry.

Soon Dorothy began crossing the walkway. "Ah, that's our hostess at Gingerbread," said Jackie. "And you must be Linda," she said to Henry's sister. "Thank you for the loan of the sandals." Renee was still wearing them, and they were still big on her.

"This is Dorothy," Renee said to Henry and Linda. "My next-door neighbor and closest friend."

"Glad to meet you," said Henry.

Dorothy said, "Well, Renee, you didn't tell me how handsome your hero was."

Dorothy was a couple of inches taller than Henry, and she towered over Renee. She had long blonde hair over a very friendly face. As the adults went into the kitchen for drinks, the four children went out to the porch. "How long have you been in New Orleans?" Renee asked Henry.

"I was born here," he said. "And you, Dorothy?"

"I'm a native as well," she answered. "How old are you, Linda?"

"Ten," said the younger girl. "My grandfather lives in the Garden District."

"Mine lives in New Iberia," said Renee. "What does your father do?"

"He works for a newspaper," said Henry. "He writes editorials."

"Let's all be friends! My dad sells hardware," said Dorothy.

"Mine is a surveyor," said Renee. "I love swimming, don't you?"

Henry said, "Love it, and bike riding."

Renee liked everything that Henry liked. That certainly made her happy. She made a move to take Henry's hand. He wasn't aware and so didn't cooperate. "Where do you live?" she finally asked.

"In Edgewood, on Clermont Drive," said Henry. "It's a long distance from North Claiborne."

That news was not so good. Renee thought about it. She wanted Henry to be her boyfriend but wasn't sure how to accomplish that. She thought back to the afternoon when Henry had massaged her foot. When she told her mother about it, she scolded her for not polishing her nails. Henry didn't seem to mind that at all. She looked at Linda. She was well groomed and self-confident. So that was the kind of girl Henry knew. Then she turned to Henry. "How long will you be here at the lake?"

"We're going home Sunday," he said.

"So are we," said Renee. "Back to the Ninth Ward."

"When can I see you again?"

"Saturday night," said Renee. "The Petersons are having a band at their camp. We would love for you and Linda to come."

Henry and Linda walked over to Gingerbread Saturday evening. The band was playing jazz music loudly. Eric and Stephanie were preparing for the trip home the next day. Henry found Renee and led her out to the porch while Linda found Dorothy's brother and sister, Gregory and Alice. "Do you have a telephone at home, Renee?" Eric asked.

"No. Do you ?"

"Yes. How are we going to see each other, or even make plans?"

"Perhaps our families could visit each other."

"I could probably get them to do that once or twice. But I would like to at least talk to you every day."

"We could write letters," Renee suggested. She had a small notebook in her pocket, wrote down her address, and gave it to Henry. He then gave her his.

"What would we write about?"

"We could write the story of how you rescued me."

"Writing stories is a good idea," said Henry. "But not about us, or anyone real. This would be something we both enjoy and share."

"That's great, Henry. Do you want to go back in?"

He shook his head."No, I want to be with you. We don't have a lot of time, and I like being this close to you."

"So what do you want to do?"

"Let's play Twenty Questions."

"Okay," she agreed. Throughout the game, they made eye contact with each other. Henry impressed Renee with his intelligence, and she impressed him with her sense of humor. He knew that even though they had shared interests, his main interest was Renee herself.

"Let's see what's going on inside," Renee finally suggested. Henry agreed.

The Gautiers invited the Kaufmanns for Thanksgiving, along with the Petersons next door. All were fairly new to the area. Eric was an only child who was second generation in the city. Stephanie was from far-off Tulsa. The Gautiers were from New Iberia, a half-day trip away. Charles Peterson had moved to New Orleans from Delaware when he was ten. He worked with his partner, Mark Fleming, in a hardware store on Almonaster Avenue. Jane, his wife, was a native, born to a German family in the upper Ninth Ward. Both were blue-eyed blonds, as were all three of their children: Dorothy, ten-year-old Gregory, and Alice, who was in kindergarten.

The Gautiers' house was designed to be a double, but nobody else lived in it. They owned it, having bought it with the proceeds from a house they'd sold in New Iberia. On the west side of the house were three bedrooms and a bathroom. On the east side were the living room, dining room, a rather large kitchen, and another bathroom. A wall separated the two sides of the house, but there was a door cut through it between the dining room and the small hall that connected the two rear bedrooms. The back bedroom was for the parents, and Renee's room was in the very front. The middle bedroom was used as a combination office and family room. There was a dining table in the kitchen where the family normally ate. The dining room was used only when the Gautiers had company.

After months of written correspondence, Henry was finally going to see Renee again. Occasionally she telephoned him from Petersons' house. The short stories they had written were only a page or two. When he finally greeted her, they sat down together in the living room. "I really like what you wrote, Renee," he began.

"And you are quite the prose artist," she replied.

"Let's write something together—something longer."

"What should we write about?"

"What interests us the most: relationships between boys and girls."

"You're still thinking of the kisses I gave you."

"Of course," he said. "But you are fascinating in so many ways."

"And you are the hero who rescued me. What could be more fascinating than that?"

Henry had never been rescued, and so he wasn't sure what to say. He remembered how surprised he was at how much he enjoyed her company that day. Jackie called them in for dinner. They sat down to roast turkey with oyster stuffing, yams, mixed greens, ham, and corn bread. They started off with a shrimp salad, and the meal was preserved for the palate with a fine claret of classic vintage. Dessert was mince pie and coffee.

After dinner, the adults went into the living room while Renee led the other children to her room. She and Dorothy had been best friends since the Gautiers had moved to New Orleans. Dorothy was a head taller than Renee. Together with Henry, they formed a group of three; Linda joined with Gregory and Alice. Dorothy put her arm around Henry and said, "Thanks to you, there are three of us here today."

"Have you ever been rescued, Dorothy?" asked Renee.

"No. Have you, Henry?"

"I'm afraid not," he replied.

"As small as Renee is, she probably couldn't carry you."

Henry responded, "Well, not the same way. But if we were in the water, she could bring me to shore. Size means a lot less in the water."

"So you're saying that if we were in the water, like out at the camp, I could rescue you?" Renee asked.

"That gives me an idea for a story," said Henry.

"All right, you authors," said Dorothy. "When do I get to provide a plot?"

"I didn't know you were interested in doing that," said Renee. "Until I met Henry, I'd never written a story."

Henry was worried about when he would get to see Renee again, so he took a bold step. "I challenge you to a race, Renee. Bicycles. Anywhere we can get together for it."

"I accept, Henry. It would be easier to get my bike to your house, with Papa's car, than for you to pedal up to my house."

"Loser buys the winner a candy bar and a soft drink."

"You can buy yourself one too."

"Oh, you think you're that good?"

"We're here now," said Dorothy. She had a deck of cards in her hand. "Let's play hearts."

Soon it was time for the Kaufmanns to leave. "Too bad you don't have a telephone, Renee," Henry lamented.

"We're getting one next month," said Renee. We'll have it by Christmas."

Both Henry and Renee were preparing for confirmation. Henry was scheduled for confirmation on Pentecost of 1927. Renee would be confirmed the following year, when the bishop visited her parish. As soon as the Gautiers had a telephone, Renee called to talk to Henry.

"Do you have to go to catechism, Henry?"

"Yes, three times a week for two years."

"We have it twice a week. Sister Agnes teaches us. We go to the church school after our own school is almost finished on Tuesday and Thursday."

"I have it with Pastor Trautmann Tuesdays and Thursdays after school, and Saturday mornings. The first year we studied the Commandments and the Creed. This year we learned the meaning of each petition of the Lord's Prayer."

"We say that too, but we don't end it like Lutherans do."

Henry replied, "Luther didn't either. I think that came with English, although when the older folks say the *Vaterunser*, they always include it in German."

"My parents hardly ever pray."

"Don't you learn Latin prayers?"

"The priests say Latin prayers. Ordinary people hardly ever do," said Renee.

"I have to visit your church sometime, and you have to visit mine."

"I would like that. But it's easier for me to visit yours because your parents always go."

They made plans for Henry's parents to pick up Renee one Sunday, take her to the worship service, and then head to their house for dinner before they brought her home. At dinner Renee had an observation. "Lutherans get up and down a lot at church."

"We stand up for the prayers, and when the Gospel is read," said Eric. "We sit for the hymns and the sermon."

"And we stand for the major parts of the liturgy," said Stephanie.

"You don't have anything to kneel on," Renee noted.

"I know what you mean," said Stephanie. "The kneelers that fold out from the pew. I think all Catholic churches have them."

"Do Lutherans ever bless themselves with the cross?" Renee asked as she touched her forehead, heart, and shoulders.

"Over at Pastor Weiser's church they do," said Eric. "Not all Lutherans practice piety the same way."

"What was that prayer you said at the beginning?"

"That was the general confession. We all say that together to confess our sins. Then the pastor pronounces the absolution; he forgives us," said Henry.

"We don't have that," said Renee. "But we can go to confession during the week."

"I'm very glad we did this," said Henry. As he said it, he resolved to ask his pastor for a book about denominational differences.

"I wish my parents knew as much about our church as you do about yours," Renee responded.

"I wish we had time to discuss this more completely," said Stephanie. "But it's getting time to take Renee home. Tomorrow is a school day."

Henry and Renee sat in the back seat. Renee sat in the middle so she could be closer to Henry, which Henry enjoyed. They both remembered the day they met at Milneburg. They thought the ride to Renee's was too short. On the way home, Henry talked to his parents about national events. They agreed that the Confederacy faced Latin America, and so most trade would be with Spanish-speaking countries. They were glad about the open border with the United States. Railroads connected their major cities. If they went far enough north, there was another open border with Canada.

Stephanie was living in New Orleans when her home territory became the state of Oklahoma. In a way, she had always been a Confederate.

Chapter Five

On the Monday before Mardi Gras, Renee was excited to get up. There would be no school, because this was part of a four day weekend. Henry was coming to her house on his bicycle, and he wasn't bringing Linda. Dorothy's mother was taking her and the younger children shopping downtown. Henry said he wanted to share story ideas with her, but Renee had another agenda. She was looking forward to the kind of intimacy she had with Henry on the day they'd met the previous June. They often talked on the telephone now, but seeing Henry face to face was bound to be a delight. She knew her mother would interrupt them frequently with all sorts of sweets, but there was a chance she could lead him to the backyard. She thought of how he had massaged her injured foot. She hadn't wanted him to put it down. She wouldn't need any kind of rescuing today, and neither was she likely to hurt herself. Faking it would be mean, a kind of deception that Henry didn't deserve. But he would be with her. She was intelligent enough to wing it from there.

Once Jacquelyn welcomed Henry into the house and he and Renee had eaten their first treat of the day, Renee said she wanted to show Henry the backyard. It was a small yard devoid of playground equipment, but it had a metal glider on which they could both sit. It was a chilly February day, but they were both warmly dressed with pants and jackets.

"So, Henry, I was thinking about the day we met."

"I remember saying that I liked you because you were a girl."

"I will never forget that," said Renee. "Neither will I forget how you took care of me."

"Could we do something like that in our story?" he asked.

"Teenagers might believe it," Renee replied, "but we also might need to do more research with it."

"You mean like asking other teenagers if they had experiences like ours?"

"Have you talked to your friends about it?"

Henry said, "Just Tommy Farley. He has never known a girl the way I know you."

"I've talked to Dorothy about it. In fact, we talk about it all the time."

Renee's dark hair and diminutive size were very attractive to Henry. He was glad to be sitting next to her. Renee could sense that Henry would probably agree to some degree of intimacy today.

"I really don't talk about you much with Linda," Henry suddenly said.

"I like Linda," said Renee.

"I feel awkward being so close to a girl. Don't get me wrong—I love being with you. I won't forget the kisses you gave me, or your parting comment."

"You mean *merci, mon ami*?"

"Only you said it much more softly. There was affection in it."

"To match the affection your fingers put into my foot," Renee replied. "I didn't have to tell you to be gentle. You just were."

"I suppose even then, I was thinking of you as very special. I couldn't say the word *girlfriend*, but today I think I can."

Renee smiled. She knew how difficult it was for him to say that. "I wish we went to the same school."

"All the other kids would talk about us. I'm glad we don't."

"My parents really like you."

"I think my parents like you. They know you're good and smart. My dad worries because you're Catholic."

"Being Lutheran is really important to him, isn't it?"

"It's probably the most important thing in his life. You really should talk to my Grandpa George sometime."

"Where does he live?" Renee asked.

"On Second Street, in the Garden District. His wife died in the yellow fever epidemic of 1901. He raised my dad along with the cook and the maid."

The conversation was turning away from intimacy. Renee wanted to navigate it back in that direction. She wanted to kiss him but doubted that he would go along with it. She rested her head on his shoulder, and she was so small that she had to practically get on his lap for that. Henry loved the attention Renee gave him. She was being more intimate than he liked, but he would never make a move that appeared to be rejecting her. He had inherited some stoicism from his half-Cherokee mother. "Renee?" he said.

"Yes, Henry?"

"Remember the challenge I offered you at Thanksgiving?"

"Refresh me."

"The bicycle race. We both have our bikes here. What route would you suggest?"

Renee was again disappointed at the turn the conversation had taken, but all she asked was, "Do you want to race now?"

"We might wait until after lunch, but let's do it then."

"How long a race do you want?"

"Maybe about fifteen minutes. Loser buys the winner a soft drink. How does that sound to you?"

Renee considered the wager for a minute. She had no problem with buying Henry a drink if he beat her, but she would rather get something more physical from him if she won. But to suggest it now might frighten him away. She agreed.

"How about down Claiborne to Alvar, out to Florida Avenue, up to Gallier, and then back here?"

"We can't buy a drink here," he answered. "Why not end the race at Delta Market? Then we can ride back here without competition."

"Is that long enough, Henry?"

"It's shorter, but I can enjoy your company close at hand without worrying about racing."

"You get a full ten points for that one." She was amazed at Henry's *savoir faire*. It made being with him even more pleasant. "We go after lunch."

Renee and Henry didn't rest very long after lunch, just enough to let the meal settle. Renee explained to Jacquelyn what they were doing, and then they moved their bikes onto North Claiborne Avenue. Renee took a quick lead as the race started. She turned onto Alvar Street, and was out of sight from Henry for about fifteen seconds. But as he turned the corner, there was a car coming. Renee had to go on the sidewalk to dodge it. Henry was about to do the same when the car turned into a driveway, and so he gained on Renee. She had to stop at Galvez Street for the traffic but got away just as Henry arrived. It took half a minute before her hero could start after her. Around Tonti Street, the pavement became very broken. Henry made better time through this, gaining on Renee. She turned onto Florida Avenue just a few seconds ahead of him.

Now the race changed. It was no longer to the swift, but to the enduring. Renee gave it all she had, but her speed gave way to Henry's endurance. He paced himself better than she had as Delta Market came into view. By Gallier Street, they were side by side. Renee hit a chuck hole, bouncing out of her seat. Henry passed her, but as soon as he saw she had stopped, he went back to see if she was all right. Renee had not fallen far, and she wasn't hurt, although her skirt was torn.

As he walked over to her, she said, "You could have won easily."

Henry picked up Renee's bike and smiled at her. "I wouldn't want to win like that," he said. "A race shouldn't be about luck."

"I know you didn't finish," Renee said, "but this has to count as winning."

"Shall we ride over to the market now?" asked Henry.

"Yes. I'm ready to buy you that drink."

"That's a good thing," Henry said as they peddled slowly up to the market. "I'm not sure I would have had enough money."

Renee stopped and walked her bike next to Henry. She looked straight ahead as she said, "But you raced me anyway?"

Henry did not really look at her as he asked, "Was I very bold?" He didn't want her to see that he was smiling.

They stopped at the door to the market. "I didn't really want the drink, you know," Renee said. "I would have bought you one if I'd won, but I really wanted a foot massage."

Henry opened the door. "That wasn't what we agreed on," he said.

"I know," Renee replied. "I wasn't thinking when I accepted the stakes." She bought the soft drink and gave it to Henry. "I still remember the day we met. You didn't think kissing my foot would make it better, but you were willing to rub it. Well, I would like to have that again—and again, and again."

Henry took a drink and thought for a moment. "I'm surprised you want your feet massaged, as ticklish as you are."

"If you do it right, it won't tickle."

Henry turned to the door. As the two walked out, Henry looked uncomfortable. He looked Renee in the eye and said, "I've never massaged anybody before."

"That's not how I remember it," Renee answered. "But we don't need to do that today. I understand you want to do the best job you can. Please promise you will learn." She looked so cute at that moment. Henry wanted to spend time with her above all. He could see how badly she wanted this. "Will you promise to do that?"

The memory was just as pleasant for Henry. "Of course I will," he replied.

The following week, Henry had been talking on the telephone with Renee about their story when she mentioned Lenten abstinence. He went into the living room where Eric was reading the paper. "Dad," he began, "it must be hard to be Catholic."

"What brings this about?" Eric asked.

"I was just talking to Renee. She told me that after Mardi Gras, they fast for forty days, not counting Sundays."

"That doesn't mean they don't eat anything, son," he said. "It means they abstain from meat twice a week and generally deny themselves something they enjoy the rest of the year."

"I'm glad we don't do that."

"Sit down, Henry."

"Now?"

"Yes, on the sofa. I want to talk to you about Renee."

Henry sat on the sofa as close to his father as he could. "You know, Dad, Renee and I can talk to each other as freely as you and I. She's intelligent, polite, and kind."

"Not so loud," said Eric, "Linda isn't old enough to think about boys yet, so I don't want her to hear us talk about this."

Henry lowered his voice. "I think of Renee as my girlfriend, Dad."

"I want you to be careful there, Henry."

"About what?"

"The difference in your faith. Don't you think you're moving pretty quickly with her?"

"Were you and Mom both Lutheran?"

"No. Remember, I met your mother in college. She hardly ever saw a church when she was growing up. Her father was a Scotch-Irish Protestant, and her mother was a Cherokee Indian."

"Wasn't your mother Catholic?"

"She was Irish, all right. She was baptized Catholic, but her family wasn't religious. Her father was a Mason. She became Lutheran when she married my father."

"Renee is Cajun, Dad. She speaks French."

"So do we, Henry. But we aren't Catholic. Have you ever talked to Renee about your faith?"

"Sometimes. So did you and Mom that day she came to church with us."

"You've never been in her church. It's dark in there. On the sides of the church, you would see these little booths that look like closets. You go in there, and the priest is already sitting on his side. Then you have to tell him all of your sins, and he gives you a penance, which is what they call absolution. To complete the transaction, you have to fulfill an assignment that the priest gives you. At that point, you have forgiveness. But it's only when you take Holy Communion that your forgiveness is sealed."

"Renee did tell me she had to go to church to confess."

"Right. That's what she was talking about."

"Is that wrong?"

"Would you like to believe that your sins aren't forgiven unless you tell them to somebody?"

"I didn't realize it was like that. It would be hard."

"These are all things you have to think about when you get close to a Catholic girl, Henry. I know how good and sweet Renee is. And your mother really loves her. I'm not telling you that you can't enjoy her company. I am saying that sooner or later, you have to talk to her about these things." This conversation upset Henry. Eric saw his discomfort, and so he told him, "There is no hurry about any of this. Just know that it's out there."

"May I be excused now?"

"Of course. Are you finished your homework?"

"I'll get back to it now." He went back to his room.

The following weekend, Maurice brought Renee to Henry's house for an afternoon visit. Eric was working that day, so Henry led Renee into the living room. "Let's go over to the sofa. I have two clipboards, so we can compare notes."

"Okay," she answered.

"What have you got so far?"

"On the Outer Banks of the Carolinas, a girl in a boat rescues a boy who swam out as the tide was changing, and he couldn't get back. They like each other right away. The girl is Catholic, and the boy is Presbyterian …"

He asked, "Do you know any Presbyterians?"

"Yes, my friend Ann. She's in my class."

"Are we going to rely more on imagination or experience?"

"We both have great imaginations, but they have to start with what we know."

"Agreed. Would you like a drink?"

"Do you have tea?" Renee asked.

"I'll get it right away. Write down these names: Mary Flanagan and George White."

Henry went to the kitchen as Renee pondered the names he had offered. She started to write something about Mary having romantic feelings, and then she checked herself. Was this imagination or experience? "Henry, would you say our relationship is romantic?"

Henry hated that question. In his own mind, it would mean crossing a line he was reluctant to reach. Still, reason had to rule. "Let's judge whether our relationship is romantic," he said.

"So you want to begin by defining terms?"

"How else?"

"Romantic relationships are between people whose main interest is in the other person, rather than in some common interest."

"That's a very good definition. I don't think I can improve on it."

"You're unbelievable, Henry. For a boy, you certainly are easy to lead."

"It sounds as though you need to tell me about the other boys you try to lead."

"I'm not the one trying to lead them. I'm talking about the boys my friends know."

"Would you like some crackers?" he offered.

"Yes."

Henry brought the tea and crackers into the living room and set them on the coffee table. "You are a good leader, Renee. It would be foolish for me not to go along with you."

"You're a good leader too."

"I must be, because I'm yet to see you challenge me."

Renee smiled. "But getting back to the story, do you know what Presbyterians teach?"

"We studied them in church history. They're Calvinists."

"I don't know what that means."

"The only thing I remember is that they were 'low church.'"

"That sounds familiar. Like iconoclasts?"

"They read the Old Testament more than the New, but they do baptize and believe in Jesus."

"It would be better if Mary and George didn't talk about church too much."

"If George's dad is like mine, it could get in the way."

"So how do they talk to each other?" Renee asked.

"So far they're still out in the ocean. Mary stops the boat to help George get in. He should say, 'It's good to see a friendly face.' Then she says …"

"'My name is Mary. What's yours?'"

He said, "That's rather prosaic. Is that what you would say?"

"I'm not the character. I would say something Catholic."

"Very well. George tells her his name and then explains why he was in trouble."

"They have a bit of a trip to the shore. Plenty of time to get acquainted."

"How old are they?"

"I think sixteen—both of them. George has his man's voice."

"And Mary is small for her age, like you."

"George is very grateful to Mary for rescuing him. And he's attracted to her as well." As she said this she leaned her head on Henry's shoulder. They stopped to eat a couple of crackers.

"The romantic aspect is important," said Henry. "That's the reason we're writing this story at all."

"Very true," said Renee. "We need to experience kissing more."

"Keep still," Henry insisted as he kissed her cheek. "Am I going in the right direction?"

"It will be some time before you arrive, But I admire your enthusiasm."

They sat apart as they heard someone coming. It was Linda. "Hi, Renee," Linda said as she sat on a hassock across the coffee table from the sofa. She picked up two crackers and ate one. "What are you two doing?"

"Working on our story," said Henry.

"Could I see it?" she asked.

"It isn't finished," said Renee. "We are going to have to get together again to finish it."

"What's it about?"

"Teenagers who have a romantic relationship," said Henry.

"A Catholic and a Protestant," added Renee. "The girl is the Catholic."

"So she has ashes on her forehead the day after Mardi Gras?" asked Linda.

"Yes," her brother replied. "That's why we call it Ash Wednesday."

Linda took another cracker. "Are you and your parents going to Milneburg this summer?" she asked Renee.

"They haven't said anything about it yet, but I'm sure we will."

"Milneburg!" said Henry. "We can simulate rescuing each other in the water. Let's put the story down until we've had a chance to do that."

"Do you want to start another one, then?" asked Renee.

"What does simulate mean?" asked Linda.

"Going through the motions of being in trouble and being rescued," Henry explained.

"I don't want to do that," said Linda.

"You don't have to," Renee replied. "I think Dorothy would join in that."

"So I'll be playing with Gregory and Alice again," Linda concluded.

Henry loved his little sister. He looked at her with those black Cherokee tresses. But he also knew she wasn't ready for the conversations he would have with Renee. "We'll do plenty of things with you too." he said. "This year you can stay up on Saturday when the band is there."

"Did Mom say that?" she asked.

"Not yet," Henry replied. "But I'll ask her very nicely."

In the summer of 1927, Henry was fourteen and Renee was thirteen. Henry looked forward to the last two weeks in July, when his family would be at Tulsa; the Gautiers and Petersons would be at Gingerbread. For two weeks, he and Renee would hardly ever be separated.

The southern side of Lake Pontchartrain was rather shallow; one had to swim out about two hundred yards to find water deeper than ten feet. That was plenty enough for the children. They would wade out as far as they could and then swim around. The rescue simulation was simple. Each of the three would be the distressed one in turn, and the rescuers would alternate. Each would rescue the other two. Renee began as the distressed, and Dorothy quickly retrieved her. Renee had already been rescued, and so not much was learned from that pairing.

Henry tried to be distressed when his turn came to be rescued, but his reflexes kept prompting him to swim. Finally, he forced himself to go limp. Renee was after him at once, turning his head to the side, throwing her left arm around his middle, swimming with her right arm, and frog-kicking with her legs. She had no trouble holding up Henry in the water. Henry succeeded in relaxing; he trusted his life to Renee, and was well rewarded for it. This sweet, lovely girl was carrying him to safety. Small though she was, she was in complete control. Henry let go and felt the overwhelming peace of being in the hands of his thirteen-year-old heroine. Henry allowed his imagination to override the simulation aspect. At last he had experienced being rescued, and he loved it.

When the simulations were over, the three teenagers climbed up on the wooden deck. There was always a pile of towels there so they could dry off. As they did, Linda, Gregory, and Alice headed for the water. Dorothy looked after them as Henry and Renee faced the south. "What's the matter out there?" Dorothy asked.

Henry and Renee looked back at the lake and noticed that Alice was having difficulty. This was no simulation. Dorothy asked Henry to go after her. He jumped off the deck back into the water and headed out toward Alice. He was amazed to see that his little sister already had the situation in hand. She had her arm around Alice and was swimming with the other arm. Henry reached them to help. Soon they were in water where Henry could stand up. He picked up Alice, who was all right, and he carried her to where all the children were able to stand. Then he picked up Linda in his arms and kissed her on the forehead. "Way to go, little sister," he said. "Today, you are a rescuer."

Linda went back to swimming with Gregory and Alice as Henry went back to the deck. Renee and Dorothy were waiting there to help him dry off. Suddenly they heard the whistle of the eastbound *Rebel*. The three hugged each other.

It was Dorothy who broke the silence. "Thanks to you, Henry, there are three of us here." The *Rebel* always reminded her of the rescue.

"About a year ago, Henry was carrying me into his parents' camp. I hadn't met Linda yet."

"I was two camps down and had no idea of what was going on. It was only when Renee came back and told us about her romantic encounter."

"Henry took very good care of me. He took the rock out of my foot, and he has such gentle hands. I'm still waiting for him to give me another foot massage."

"I would like that too," Dorothy injected, sitting back on the deck and lifting up her foot.

Henry noticed that now a second girl was expressing a desire to enjoy his fingers.

"So Henry," Renee said, "do you like Dorothy because she's a girl too?"

Henry reflected on that question. He had a special affection for Renee, but he wanted to be Dorothy's friend. For that matter, he loved Linda and had yet another kind of affection for her. They were all girls. "Girls are wonderful," he said. "Each of you is special to me, but not all in the same way. You need a boyfriend, Dorothy."

"Would your friend Tommy Farley like Dorothy?" asked Renee.

"When can I meet him?" asked Dorothy.

Henry replied, "Would you believe this Friday? He's coming to the camp to visit me." He took the foot Dorothy was holding up and gave her big toe a firm pinch. Dorothy put her foot back on the deck.

"Where does he go to school?" she asked.

"At John McDonogh High. He lives across the street from me."

"Does he like girls?"

Henry knew that his own hormones were directing him toward the fairer sex. He was sure Tommy was facing the same internal revolution. "I would bet he does," he said.

Renee injected. "It's up to you, Dorothy."

Chapter Six

Henry had turned sixteen the previous January; Renee had turned fifteen in May. They had talked on the telephone several times a week, visited each other when they could, and spent a very enjoyable fortnight at the camp. At the end of October, however, both families had their attention turned to an economic catastrophe: the Crash of 1929. Although Eric's job was secure, his editorials had a somber tone. Maurice had finished his bridge project at Pointe-aux-Herbes, and he now worked for the state. Stephanie had never really worked, but now with Henry and Linda in their teens, her income would be more important than her homemaking. Neither family had moved since they had first met in 1926. Henry was a junior at John McDonogh High School, and Renee was a sophomore at Francis T. Nicholls.

Neither Henry nor Renee had an automobile. They both had bicycles, but normally traveled around the city by streetcar; it was only five cents and stopped every two blocks. They had finished the story about George and Mary and had begun collaboration on another. The Great Depression was falling in every place, yet neither of their families had suggested they get jobs, which were not easy to get.

Henry loved Renee. There was no other way to say it. He had outgrown youthful infatuation. Although he had a common interest with her in their stories, their stories were reflections of their own experience. Whether they had that common interest or not, Henry would still want to be with Renee. Other boys tried to persuade him that he should be trying to have sex with the girl, with no interest beyond that. Henry did not understand that attitude. What the other boys said was only natural was something evil to Henry. Nature was no longer an ally of mankind. Before the Fall, Adam and Eve lived in the natural world. That world disappeared with the *Ursünde*. What appeared to be only natural to his acquaintances was subnatural to Henry. Like most Lutherans, he totally rejected Darwinism, considering it rather silly. The natural world was Eden, a vegetarian, nudist, patriarchal paradise where it was always summer. That was God's intention for man. What everything had become was subnatural and distorted nature— a world of pain, pride, and every other deadly sin.

He knew he had no choice but to live in it, but he definitely did not belong to it. He was born again of water and the Spirit, and thus he had internalized the Word of God, and was transformed by it. He sinned of course. He was human. He was a son of Adam. But he knew when he was sinning, at least most of the time, and he confessed it to God. On Sunday he heard the pastor speak the completely objective words of the absolution. He understood God's forgiveness to be absolutely real. It was then up to him to survive in the evil, subnatural world as best he could. He tried hard not to judge the other boys, but reason demanded that he see them as inferior as far as sexual attitudes were concerned. They could not understand him, and neither could he understand them. He was ambivalent about democracy. He knew that in the fallen world, society needed checks and balances. But he did not trust the majority because the regenerate were a minority. Nevertheless, history had taught the horrors of being ruled by the saints. He knew he would be a wise ruler and would want to be kind, but experience would make him so bitter that he would become cruel. It was already happening in high school.

He could never be cruel to Renee. He knew how intelligent and reasonable she was. Henry was sure that Renee regarded him with equal respect and affection. He remembered the day they first met, when she had given him the circle of kisses on his cheek. She displayed constant devotion to him. He treasured every moment he spent with her.

One Saturday when she was visiting him, Henry said," "I have a surprise for you, Renee."

"Do you really?"

"Yes. Come over to the sofa." He led her by the hand, seated her on one end, and then sat on the other. "Now give me your foot."

Renee smiled broadly. "Are you going to massage my feet, Henry?"

"I'm not saying. But I do want your foot."

Renee took off her shoes and put her feet in Henry's lap. "Did you learn how to do it right?" she asked.

Henry produced a small bottle of lotion from his pocket. He started to take off Renee's sock. It took him a minute to get it over her heel, but soon his fingers were working her sole. "I've been practicing with Linda. It took me a while to get it right."

"Thank you, Linda," said Renee. "This really is a surprise. I've been waiting for it for more than three years."

After a few minutes, he took off her other sock and focused on giving her other foot the same attention. Renee giggled, and Henry stopped. "Did that tickle?" he asked.

"Not at all," Renee replied. "You're giving me what I've wanted for a long time. I don't want you to stop."

"That's what I expected," said Henry.

"When I've had enough, I'll say what I told you when I left you the day we met."

"That would bring back a beautiful memory," he said. "But what if I haven't had enough?"

"You mean you're enjoying this too?"

"Definitely." Her feet were still very small, delicate, and sensitive. He was used to Renee's diminutive size. She was petite in every way.

"Well, when I tell you that, it will be up to you when you want to stop. I won't object to a little extra attention."

Henry went back to Renee's first foot. "Do the other girls like this kind of thing?"

"They don't really say much about what they do with their boyfriends. I do believe we're more monogamous than other kids." She sighed as Henry's finger pressed her reflex point. "I know you're more monogamous than other boys."

"My parents and my sister really like you," Henry replied. "My dad wishes you were a Lutheran. Other than that, he's fine with you."

"My parents never talk about church," said Renee. "They attended for a while when I was getting ready for confirmation. Since then, it's as if I graduated."

Henry looked at Renee's face. She no longer wore the short hair; now it was in a ponytail. "You are beautiful," he said softly. "How did you know I was so fond of ponytails?"

"There was a girl from Honduras in my class. She had one."

"We do have a number of Latin Americans moving to New Orleans. I think that's one reason the Depression hasn't reached us yet."

"I thought it had."

"It's much worse in most other places," said Henry.

"So tell me, does Linda enjoy this as much as I do?"

Fried Oyster Sandwich

"She told me she liked it." He picked up Renee's second foot again. As Henry's fingers stroked her nerve endings, she gave a deep sigh. "She never sighed like that."

"Maybe she just sighed on the inside. Is she here?"

"She's up in her room. Do you want me to call her?"

"That's okay. This could put me to sleep. I never expected that."

"I know how to wake you up."

"Don't. I would rather we were quiet for a while."

That idea was fine with Henry. Renee stayed awake, and Henry focused on massaging her until eventually she said, *"Merci, mon ami."* She said it just as softly as the day they'd met. Henry put her feet down and moved over to where she was sitting.

"I certainly didn't expect this," she said. "Is your dad going to drive me home?"

"Of course," said Henry. "But please stay for cake and coffee."

"That sounds good. Do I need to put on my shoes and socks?"

"You don't have to," he said. "Are you cold?"

"Not at all," she said. "I can't go barefoot at home. My mother insists that I paint my nails. Do you want me to paint my nails?"

"Linda sometimes paints hers. You don't have to though."

"My parents never mind when I'm with you," she said. "They trust you. They know you care about me. And they think you're a good influence on me."

Henry stood up and gave Renee his hand to help her up. He gave her a very firm hug. He couldn't imagine a sweeter moment.

Henry's grandfather's health was beginning to fail. Olivia had retired to stay with her cousins, and Essie was the only person who lived in George's house with him. She was very competent, but eventually Stephanie realized that her presence there would be required. She did not drive, so she would go on the streetcar on Tuesday morning and return home on Thursday evening. She and Eric would go there together on Sunday. Henry and Linda usually went with them, except when there was a church youth social.

Henry spoke to Renee on the telephone almost every day. She was certainly aware of the difficulty with Grandpa George, and so she wanted to visit Henry's house to help raise his morale. Linda was Renee's friend by now as well. Henry knew that Renee had become a woman but did not think about it that much. She was still the girl on the railroad track by the camp four years ago, but a little taller and with a ponytail.

The house on Second Street had become a topic of family conversation. No one wanted to live there. When Grandpa George would die, it would be empty. Eric and Stephanie knew the neighborhood but did not want to live in the Garden District. Essie could never afford the house and did not need it because she had a house of her own on Banks Street. One option would be to rent it out. To keep it in the family was impractical. It would be seven years before Henry could live independently, and ten before Linda could. If she married early, the house would be a fine wedding gift, but meanwhile Eric and Stephanie would have to pay the taxes on it. Linda was thirteen at this time and was in no hurry to marry. The best option appeared to be to sell it. It was very attractive as a residence. Ties with the old house would be cut. Part of Eric's life would be out of his reach. Another part was just coming into view: he bought a new Packard.

Henry wanted to know more about Renee's church, and she wanted to know more about his. He prevailed on Jacquelyn to take him to the

Gautiers' church with Renee. Maurice would have none of it. Now both children had seen the similarities as well as the differences. Jacquelyn took him to the Gautier house for Sunday dinner. As they finished the main course and served the coffee, Henry addressed the topic.

"It looks as though Catholics make up a majority of the population here."

"You're right," said Jacquleyn. "Even among the colored people. And there is a large Irish neighborhood between the business district and the Garden District."

"My grandmother was born there," said Henry.

"Your grandmother Kaufmann?"

"Yes. My grandmother Weaver was a Cherokee Indian."

"Most of the Protestants came from Virginia in the 1830s," said Renee.

"They were Tidewater people," said Henry, "Episcopalians. But in 1839, a large number of German Lutherans arrived here. Five ships set sail from Bremen, but the *Amalia* sank. The *Olbers, Copernicus, Johann Georg,* and *Republik* all arrived safely."

"Was that a big group?" asked Jacquelyn.

"Much bigger than what stayed," said Henry. "Most of them migrated up the river to Missouri, which of course was part of the same nation then. But the group that stayed was large enough to beget a decent German community, mostly downtown."

"Were all the Germans Lutherans?" asked Renee.

"In that particular wave, they were. They were looking for religious toleration. Their country had become part of Prussia when their king died. The Prussians had a blend of Lutheran and Reformed Protestants. They wanted all of their Protestants to adopt the same practices. This group emigrated rather than comply."

"So there were other waves of Germans?"

"Yes. There were German Catholics, German Methodists, and German Evangelicals. Those were the ones who accepted the Prussian-style union."

"What do you mean by toleration?" asked Renee.

"Technically, it means each group allows the others to exist and shows a measure of respect. In that regard, it's a *quid pro quo*. Religions don't necessarily approve of the ones they tolerate; they still try to proselytize from them. But they only do that in private, not in business, politics, or society."

Renee said, "I think they read the Bible a lot more in your church than in mine."

"I heard it read in yours today. It seemed strange to hear it in Latin."

"I see both churches have baptismal fonts."

"Yes. We both believe in baptismal regeneration; we both believe in an educated clergy who make up the teaching office, and we both believe that one must interpret the Bible according to the rule of faith."

"Then why don't our churches get along better?" Jacquelyn asked.

"I might say because of people like my father, but that's dodging the question. We believe that sinners are justified by faith, while your church teaches they are justified by faith and good works. As for the practices of piety, such as Marian devotion, the Rosary, and the like, almost everyone knows which of these are Catholic."

"So you and I have to be like the Montagues and Capulets?" asked Renee.

"I would hate to see it come to that," said Henry. "I might have to choose between you and my father. That would be dreadful."

"Do you think it would come to that?" asked Renee.

"We're still in high school, Renee. We know we want to be together. Down the road, I can see us making a home together. We would face some hard questions then."

"You're a year ahead of me. Will you stay nearby?"

"I already know I can attend Tulane University," he said. "Have you been thinking about college?"

"I know I want to go, but I don't have one picked out yet," she replied.

"Will my parents be okay with our being together? My mother certainly would, and Dad likes you. He really likes you. He thinks you're beautiful, as well as intelligent and poised. Keep impressing him like that."

Henry graduated from McDonogh High School in 1931 as the salutatorian. He lived at home and commuted daily to the university. He talked to Renee when he could, but school demanded most of his time.

At Thanksgiving that year—which was at Grandpa George's—as the family gathered in the living room after dinner together with the Gautiers, Henry proposed to Renee. She accepted graciously, which caused the entire ensemble to break out in cheers. Eric did not feel the joy he showed.

Maurice could see that Eric had some misgivings. "I'm certainly glad my daughter is marrying her hero," he said.

"I'm glad they're both happy," said Eric. "But where will they live? What will be their religion? Can they split themselves between two churches?"

"I know," said Maurice. "I'm glad Jackie and I didn't have to face that. Let me tell you something. Renee told us at the beginning of the school year that she knew this was going to happen. She said she wanted to attend your church."

"Did she say why?"

"Yes. She said if it attracts you and Stephanie every Sunday, it must have something that Jackie and I can't find in our own tradition. She wants to please you very much. We both know she's the perfect mate for Henry."

"That is wonderful news," said Eric. "What happens next?"

"Renee has to finish high school," said Maurice. "From that point on it's up to them, isn't it?"

Stephanie called the men for dessert and coffee. Everyone celebrated. Finally, Linda asked Renee if she could be the maid of honor. Renee told her she was planning to ask Dorothy to do that, but that she would certainly be in the wedding party. "But I owe you a lot," Renee added. "You helped teach Henry how to give foot massages. Everyone should have such a skillful sister-in-law."

The following spring, Renee graduated from Francis T. Nicholls High School as the valedictorian. There was a party at the Gautiers' house, which Henry and Renee left after about an hour to sit in her room.

"At last," she said. "After all that standing, you can massage my poor feet."

"I'm happy for you, Renee," he said. "But there is one thing I would like to get off my chest."

"First take off my pumps," she said.

Henry took her feet in his lap and with a little difficulty removed the shoes from Renee's feet, which were somewhat swollen from standing. "Now," he said, "there was one part of your address that I found somewhat embarrassing."

"Because I referred to when you rescued me?" she asked.

"That's right," he said. "I'm very glad it happened, all right? But I didn't do it for credit."

Renee pulled her stockings down to her knees and then motioned for Henry to remove them the rest of the way. She was lying down now. "I said that I would not be giving that address if it were not for the gallant boy who put himself in harm's way to save me. I didn't say your name."

Henry removed Renee's stockings while he said, "Linda knew who you meant. In fact, I think everybody did."

"So what's wrong with that?" asked Renee. "Everything that has happened with us started with your heroic action." She sighed as Henry massaged her foot.

"There's really nothing wrong with it. I guess I'm just sensitive about it."

"I'm not sorry I praised you. Henry. But I am sorry I embarrassed you. Go ahead and tickle my foot. I deserve it."

"Renee, darling, I don't get any pleasure from annoying you. When can I see you next?"

"Can you come to my house next Saturday?" she asked.

"You couldn't keep me away," Henry replied smiling.

"I'm going to make you a delicious shrimp and oyster gumbo, like the kind my grandmother makes in New Iberia."

"I'm so glad I'm marrying you," said Henry.

Part III
WOPR

Chapter Seven

In 1936, Henry was twenty-three years old with a degree in classical languages and a minor in journalism. He had married Renee, who turned twenty-two in May. Henry began working for his father's newspaper when a new venture opened up before him: the paper's own radio station.

There were many immigrants from the United States, which was still in the throes of the Great Depression. In New Orleans, there was employment, and it was also the gateway to Latin America, where there were many more opportunities for those who spoke the language. The petroleum industry was thriving, the salt and sulfur mines always needed workers, and wholesale grocers, sugar refineries, and coffee production had openings. A young radio journalist came down from Chicago and entered Henry's office on a morning in late March for an interview. His name was Stanley Kozar.

The radio station's offices and studios were just north of the downtown area in the Jung Hotel. Henry took the Frenchman streetcar to Canal Street and then transferred to the Canal out to the Jung. It was about a thirty-minute trip. There were diners along Canal Street where lunch could be reasonably bought. Henry took only half an hour for lunch so he could leave by 3:00 p.m. He wanted to be with Renee. The call letters of the station were chosen as an acrostic. Although they had no choice about the W, the OPR stood for Orleans Parish Radio.

Henry got off the Frenchman streetcar at Prieur Street and walked four blocks east and one block north to the house he and Renee had bought on Johnson Street, just east of St. Roch Park. Renee welcomed him as he came. He took off his homburg to put it on the hat rack near the front door. It was like the house where Renee had grown up, but with smaller alleys on each side of it. Renee gave him a tight hug, which he answered with a loving kiss. She still had the ponytail and short bangs. Because she was a foot shorter than Henry, he lifted her slightly as he kissed her. "I love you," he said softly.

Jacquelyn was still there for her daily visit. Henry hadn't seen her for a while, and so he asked how Maurice was doing.

"He's still working for the state, building a bridge over Bayou St. John. How are Eric and Stephanie?"

"They still have Linda at home. They're pretty busy these days."

"Do you ever see your father at work?"

Henry replied, "No, Mama Jackie. He's over at the paper, and I'm at the station on the fourth floor of the Jung Hotel."

"Did you have a good lunch today?" asked Renee.

"Stanley and I ate at Fazio's Diner," said Henry, "our usual lunchtime haunt. He had a roast beef sandwich with mayonnaise and lettuce. After four months, he still doesn't know how to pronounce that condiment."

"And what did you have, dear?"

"My favorite; the fried oyster sandwich."

"Where does Stanley live?" asked Jackie.

"On Touro Street, just below Esplanade Avenue."

"And he's single," added Renee, "so we have to arrange for him to meet Dorothy."

Fried Oyster Sandwich

"Shall we have coffee?" asked Henry.

"It's time for me to go," said Jackie. "Maurice will be home in an hour."

"Good afternoon, then," said Henry. As she left, he turned to Renee. "Linda was at the station today. I think she would like to work there part time."

"That would be great," said Renee. "Do you have anything for her to do?"

"I was thinking about the noon hour."

"I have to remember to tune in, then," she said.

Two typewriters sat facing away from each other at opposite ends of a rectangular table. Stanley sat at one of them, and Henry hovered over the other. There was a constant chattering by the Associated Press teletype. This was the newsroom, where Henry and Stanley prepared the copy, which would go on the air. The world situation had deteriorated since the calm days of the previous decade.

"What's going on?" asked Stanley.

"There's a complication with India's independence movement. Conflict between Hindus and Muslims. The Soviets are still in their second five-year plan. It doesn't appear that they're going bankrupt."

"Let's look at the teletype," said Stanley.

"Read the first thing you see."

"You'll love this one, Henry. Dynastic trouble in Germany."

"With the Bavarians?"

"How'd you guess? Princess Marcia is engaged to Grand Duke John of Luxembourg."

"Aha! A vassal of the Hapsburgs."

"Since the 1480s. That makes some competition between Germany and Austria. They were allies back in the Great War."

"Anything from France?"

"Hold on." Stanley read silently until the teletype changed the subject. "There we are. The trade unions are demonstrating against the government. It seems they were agitated by agents of Comintern."

"We need to do a special on North America," said Henry. "I was thinking about the migration patterns between the sister republics. I would also like to work on the possibility of a common currency."

"The Union is more industrial," said Stanley. "There is more opportunity for employment there."

"There are fewer black immigrants now since Illinois and Indiana repealed their anti-Negro laws. Due to the Depression, a lot of people are moving around, hoping it's better somewhere."

"Let's wrap this up quickly," said Stanley. "It's getting to be time for the sports."

"I'll keep watching the teletype for a while," Henry replied.

The teletype was chattering about Jerry Muldoon. He was the opportunist waiting to step into a power vacuum caused by Governor Huey Long's decision to run for president; 1937 would be a gubernatorial election year. Muldoon belonged to the Progressive Party. He had come from Shreveport, where he began his career as a city councilman, and then he moved on to the state legislature. Long's party, the Regular

Democrats, were becoming a minority. It appeared that Long's brother, Earl, would be Muldoon's opponent.

"Where does the Progressive Party get its money?" asked Stanley.

"From the oil companies," Henry answered. Stanley waved as he opened the door. As he left, a porter came to the door with a message for Henry. It was from the Domino Sugar Company, buying advertising time. Henry gave him a tip. He went to the long table again and saw his sister coming in.

"So this is where you work," she said.

"This is the newsroom," Henry replied. "The studio and producer's booth are through that door over there. On the other side of the hall from where you came in is the break room. And had you turned right instead of left, you would have come to the room where bands play live music on the air. Welcome to WOPR."

"So will I be working for the *Picayune*, then?" she asked.

"No, for WOPR. We're not quite independent of the paper yet, but I will be signing your checks."

"Great. What do you want me to do?"

"I want you on the air from noon to 1:00 p.m. Monday through Friday. I want you to conduct interviews with local women, and with merchants who deal with local women. If there's a news item that would interest women, have a guest on to talk about it. Use this room for scheduling and writing your on-air copy. Can you start next Monday?"

"I would love to."

Henry asked, "Did I hear Dad say that Uncle Danny is coming next summer?"

"That's right. He has a summer off before he begins his new training."

"You mean he's staying in the army?"

"Yes, but not in the cavalry. Horses are no longer efficient in military service; they're being replaced by various types of machinery. He is transferring to the flying corps. In September he begins pilot training."

"That figures. He always was the independent type. Up in the air, he will be freer."

Linda replied, "He is in his forties now. Half of his life he's been in the Yankee army."

"Well, as much as I love Uncle Danny, I need to talk to you about Dorothy Peterson. Would you like some coffee?"

"Sure."

"Go over to the break room; you'll find some cups and a pot. Then come sit next to me."

While Linda was getting her coffee, Henry checked the teletype. It was talking about football, and so he clipped the reports and put them by Stanley's chair. When she returned and sat down, Henry began. "You know how long Dorothy has been a friend with Renee and me. In high school she was active in theatre. She was very versatile: acting, props, lighting, even some assistant directing. But her forte was costumes. She designed them, acquired them, made them, fitted them, and kept them after the show was over. Soon, that hobby became a vocation."

"That's how she got to Boutique Bienville."

"She was working at Lerner's on Canal Street for a while, but eventually she found a partner with whom she could start a retail establishment of her own."

"That would be Elizabeth," said Linda.

"Yes. She has the house on Claiborne Avenue to herself now. Her parents moved to Chalmette, taking Alice with them. Gregory is married now and living in Slidell."

"You still see her every week, don't you?"

Henry said, "She visits Renee and me every Wednesday for dinner. After dinner, we go for a walk in St. Roch Park."

"Well, between us, dear brother, we can get her on the air."

"That's just what I was hoping."

That summer passed quickly. The family enjoyed what time they could at the camp, but Henry had to spend a lot of time at the station. It was a presidential year for politics, but the following year would be a gubernatorial race. Jerry Muldoon would be running, which was one thing Henry could not stand. He and his father were discussing the possibility of a third political party in Louisiana. Under President Harry Byrd, there had been a lot of industrialization. Hydroelectric plants were built on the Tennessee River. The Democratic Party had nominated John Hollings Bankhead, the governor of Alabama, who was expected to continue that trend. The Progressive Party had not yet convened, but Louisiana's own Huey P. Long had thrown his hat into the ring. Inside the state, his party was called the Regular Democrats, but he had no party in the rest of the Confederacy. He had resigned as governor to run, but he was no more tasteful to Henry than Muldoon.

"Don't look at me, Henry," said Eric. "I'm perfectly happy being an editor. That's plenty enough public life for me."

"Of course not," laughed Henry. "If anything, I would want Mom to run."

"Now *that* would be news," said Eric. "She always was a trailblazer for women."

"Would she count as being from Oklahoma?"

"It's been thirty years since she lived there. She's from here now."

"What about Mr. Salvatore?"

"He's ready to retire. I do agree with you about needing another party, at least within the state. We can't do anything about presidents, but we could be ready for next year."

"Do you think Mom would like to run the new party?" Henry asked.

"She raised you and Linda. It can't be as hard as that. But why don't you ask her?"

"I'll do an editorial about it and see what responses come in."

"Spoken like a journalist," said Eric.

The new year brought some interesting developments. In January, Renee revealed to Henry that she was pregnant. Even though she was not yet showing, she started to buy maternity clothes. She also wanted to pair Dorothy with Stanley. Henry had hired another announcer, Jerry Klauss, who played music until 10:30 p.m. when WOPR signed off. Henry arrived at the station at 7:00 a.m. to play a couple of syndicated shows, reading the news every hour until noon and commenting on it, with a couple of interviews in between. Linda went on the air at noon as Henry and Stanley went to lunch. Henry and Stanley worked together until 3:00 p.m., when Henry left for the day and Stanley turned to sports. Stanley left at 7:00 when Jerry came on.

By 4:00 p.m., Henry would be home, and Renee eagerly greeted him.

"So what did Jackie buy for the nursery today?" Henry began.

"Are you saying my mother is spoiling us? I'm not letting her take over, you know."

"It's true that we probably couldn't afford those things on our own. Just as I'm glad that Mom and Dad have us for Sunday dinner."

"Speaking of our parents," Renee said, leading in a new direction. "What is the baby going to call them? They can't both be Grandma and Grandpa."

"Why should that be difficult? Maurice and Jackie can be Grandmère and Grandpère."

"That would distinguish them. We can always fall back on that, at least."

Renee brought Henry a glass of wine and joined him by the coffee table. Henry took a sip and then said, "Linda is working at WOPR over the noon hour. She seems to like it."

"Good. What's she doing?"

"I was hoping she could get interviews with local women, but we have copy to fall back on. She could play syndicated news records. Also, I'm trying to negotiate for that soap opera my mother likes so much."

"We'll still have Saturdays to visit. She and I like to go to Dorothy's shop."

"Does she carry maternity clothes?"

"She has a small department with a fair variety. But it's fun, even if we don't buy anything."

"You think Jackie would like to be called Grandmère?

Renee grinned. "She would be happy to be called that. It's being old enough to be one that might bother her."

"And Linda will be Aunt Linda."

"She'll love that. She can babysit for us."

"So when is dinner?" Henry asked.

"It's in the oven. Should be ready around 5:30."

That evening, Henry and Renee went into the living room to listen to the radio. Renee put her foot in Henry's lap. "Hang on," he said. "I'll get the lotion."

"Being pregnant has many disadvantages. My feet still don't approve of it," Renee quipped.

"But you do get extra attention," Henry responded. "Whether it's strange snacks, cute gifts, or extra massages."

"Make this one extra long," she said as Henry sat down again. "I will always be grateful to Linda for helping you learn this."

"You control how long your massages are," said Henry as he slipped off Renee's slipper sock, which she had put on after her bath. "I would not stop without your lovely verbal cue."

"You are definitely a hands-on husband. Did you want to talk about work?"

"Not really. I was thinking about when we were in high school, and how hard it was for us to visit each other."

"Right. And the bicycle race we had."

"And the stories we wrote."

"We are truly blessed. God has been very good to us."

"He planned it that way in eternity," he said as she gave a deep sigh.

"Would you do this for Geneviève Marchand?" Renee suddenly asked.

"How do you know about her? We only mentioned her on the news once."

"I read about her in *Time*," Renee replied. "She was leading a march of French women who want the right to vote."

"Yes, in Paris."

"Along the Boulevard, from the Place Vendôme to the Place d'Étoile. That's quite a walk."

"Something about her name … you know, her surname is the French translation of mine."

"Could she be a distant relative?"

"Must be on Mom's side," Henry said.

"She isn't Cherokee."

"No, but she is a feminist. Is that close enough?

Renee smiled.

At one of his Sunday visits to his parents, Henry brought up the subject of an alternative to Muldoon and the Longs. "How do we begin something like this?" he asked.

"Take a look at possible constituencies," said Eric.

"For instance," Stephanie contributed, "Jerry Muldoon and his Progressives are spokesmen for the oil companies."

"And the Regular Democrats represent the old agricultural Louisiana," said Eric.

"The building trades are having a real growth spurt right now," said Henry. "That means Maurice is getting plenty of work. Do they have a political home?"

Eric replied, "Right now, they generally vote Progressive. Have you gotten any mail about this?"

"So far I have presented one editorial on the subject. I did get some mail from an import company. They suggested that I look to the maritime interests."

"That's a great idea," said Stephanie.

"Sounds like a start," agreed Renee.

"In ancient Athens, there was a Shore Party that looked to those interests," said Eric. "The Hill and the Plain Parties were rather like our Regulars and Progressives. It's not as though there was a one-to-one correspondence—too many variables. But we can learn a lot from the ancients."

"I would think the farmers would back the Progressives, because they like equipment that requires gasoline," said Renee.

"There are many kinds of farmers," said Eric. "The large farmers vote Progressive. But farmers who rent their land are hard pressed. Few of their children attend school past the sixth grade."

"This was a very bad spring for the strawberry farmers in the Florida parishes," noted Henry. "They need large families because they can't afford employees. But they have to feed them."

"Is there any kind of women's issue on the table?" Eric asked, looking at Stephanie.

"We vote in Louisiana," she replied. "If we had a Confederacy-wide party, that could be an issue."

"I doubt there could be a national policy on that issue," said Eric. "After all, the *raison d'être* of the Confederacy is to allow states to regulate their own polity. Now in the United States, where there are presidential elections, that would be an issue."

"We're the ones who follow the US Constitution in the way we choose a chief executive," said Stephanie.

"The *original* US Constitution," said Henry. "A lot of the unpleasantness of the last century was caused by the Twelfth Amendment."

"That's right," said Stephanie. "After that, it was all downhill."

They quieted down to eat for a few minutes, and then Renee had another question. "What about the religious division—the Catholic South and the Protestant North? Could that be a source of partisan alignment?"

"That hasn't worked for a while," said Stephanie.

"You really know your state, Mother," said Henry. "But I think the main divisions are rural versus urban, and industrial versus agricultural, at least for the present time."

"That's why we should begin with a Shore Party," said Eric.

Henry talked about these things with Stanley in the news room. Stanley added another possible constituency: the factory workers. "Just look around New Orleans," he said. "We have cement workers, coffee workers, oil refineries, sugar refineries, breweries, cotton mills …" He hadn't quite finished when they heard the teletype machine. Henry retrieved the copy. "Just something about Mexico," he said.

"That could be ours too," said Stanley. "The whole Latin American trade is part of the maritime interests."

"Like imports and exports," said Henry. "And commercial fishing. Dock workers are wage workers too. This could be a gold mine."

"Isn't it great to be on the radio?" said Stanley

In September Renee's baby was due. She was a small woman, so it was important that the baby come on time. So far she had not had a difficult pregnancy, in spite of what she said about her feet. Henry had invited her to come to work with him, but his hours were too early for her, and she frequently needed the bathroom.

Her labor began on a day when Jackie had a dental appointment. Around 1:00 in the afternoon, Henry got a call at the station. Renee needed a ride to Mercy Hospital. There was no direct transit route, and neither was Renee capable of walking to it. Henry was on the air and couldn't very well step away. He asked Stanley if he could pick up Renee; Stanley had an appointment with an advertiser. Henry told Renee to stay where she was until he could find a way to get to her.

He had an eight-minute recording of an Associated Press item, which gave him time to call Linda. Linda didn't drive, but she immediately called Dorothy, who did. Dorothy left Boutique Bienville in care of Elizabeth and went to Henry and Renee's house. Linda took the streetcar and met Dorothy there. Renee's contractions were becoming more frequent. Linda called the hospital while Dorothy helped Renee get her things together. Then Linda called the station to tell Henry that they could get Renee to the hospital. He agreed to meet them there. Henry was able to complete his program, but immediately afterward, he was in his car on his way to Mercy Hospital, which was a bit closer to the Jung than it was to his house.

Fried Oyster Sandwich

Renee was in a labor room when he arrived, and her water had broken. He massaged the small of her back. Dorothy went back to work. Linda called Jackie and then Stephanie. Henry gave thanks to God for letting the child come on time. Renee had been given a sedative, so she wasn't always making sense.

Around 6:00 p.m., a nurse examined Renee and then told the visitors it was time to take Renee to delivery. Henry and Linda kissed her, left her with the nurse, and headed to a waiting room. Within ten minutes, Maurice and Jackie joined them. Henry went down to a gift shop to buy Renee a bouquet. When he returned, Linda went to supper at the hospital snack bar. The Gautiers had relatives in New Iberia who had children, but this would be the first baby in the Kaufmann family since Linda, twenty-one years ago.

As time went by, Henry began to worry. He thought the labor was taking rather long, although this was not unusual for first children. He started to pace up and down. Jackie saw his concern and started to say her rosary. Maurice went outside to smoke. When Linda returned, she told Henry he should get something to eat, but his nerves were not capable of it. Linda gave him a hug and led him to a chair, where she could sit next to him. After a minute, he walked over to the water fountain and then came back next to his sister. In his heart, he spoke the Psalms he knew best, especially *Levavi oculis*, to which he returned several times. "The Lord shall preserve thee from all evil, He shall preserve thy soul. The Lord shall preserve thy going out and thy coming in ..."

Around 7:30, the doctor entered the waiting room. "Well, Mr. Kaufmann, you have a healthy daughter," he said.

"How's Renee?" Henry asked.

"She's a hardy little lady. It took a bit out of her, but she should be fine in a few hours. Give her a little time, and then I'm sure she'll be glad to get that bouquet."

"And the baby?" he asked.

"She's on her way to the nursery. You will see her in a bassinet there."

The whole family gave thanks to God.

The next morning, Henry and Jackie were visiting Renee in her hospital room. "Now Julia and Claudia have a little cousin," Renee said, referring to her cousin's children in New Iberia. "So, Henry, should we name her after Geneviève Marchand?"

"Nobody would know what the name was about," Jackie replied.

"Let's backtrack a minute," said Henry. "Think about the ancient dynasties. You know what comes after Julia and Claudia?"

"What?"

"Flavia. It's a beautiful name."

"How do you spell it?" asked Jackie.

"F-L-A-V-I-A," said Henry.

"It sounds Italian, even with the long *A*," said Renee.

"It's Roman. That's ancient Italian."

"It does have a pleasant sound. But I don't know anyone else named Flavia."

"We can't tell what color her hair is going to be yet," said Henry. "But if you need an association, what about the heroine in *The Prisoner of Zenda*?"

"I haven't read that," said Renee. "But I intend to."

"Before we decide, let me see what my mother thinks of it. I know my father will think it's too Italian."

Fried Oyster Sandwich

"My father will see how it goes with Julia and Claudia. He'll like it."

Henry asked, "Would you like Linda to be the godmother?"

"Definitely. How about my cousin, Hébert, for the godfather?"

"Of course, that is assuming they're willing to do it. At least we're in agreement," said Jackie.

Just then, Linda entered the room. Henry kissed Renee good-bye and went back to the station. Renee asked Linda to be the godmother, and she quickly assented.

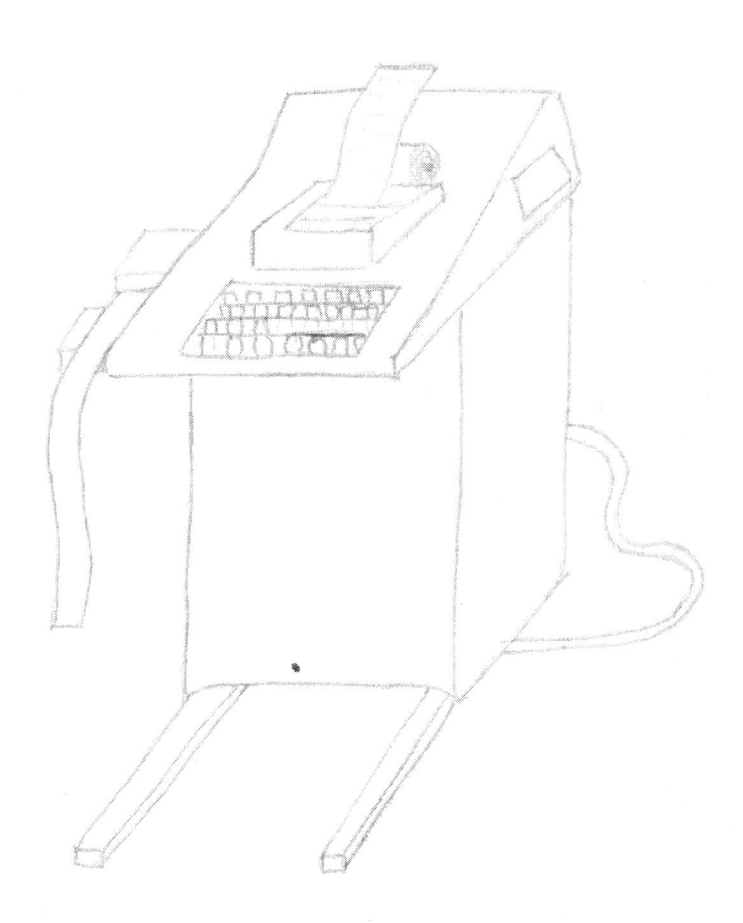

Chapter Eight

Renee had a bee in her bonnet. She wanted to pair Dorothy with Stanley. Henry would have to steer Stanley in the right direction. As soon as Flavia was old enough to take on the streetcar, Renee bundled her up and went to Dorothy's shop. Renee would have to use her diplomatic skills with a woman with whom she had grown up, and from whom little was hidden. On her first visit, she mainly talked about clothes, dropping an occasional hint that Dorothy needed somebody for whom she could get dressed up. Dorothy was interested in Renee's experience with pregnancy, which became a conversational gold mine. Flavia was a hit not only with Dorothy but also with Elizabeth, the junior partner who was using part of her wages to buy a share of the shop. Renee watched that relationship carefully; Elizabeth could become an ally in winning Dorothy over to dating Stanley.

Stanley had met Dorothy at the station, when Henry had her as a guest during his morning interviews. Sometimes he had Linda on with her to help him ask the right questions. He sold her advertising time. Dorothy was committed to upscale merchandise. She made annual trips to Dallas and Charleston, and she had even visited Paris to see the house of Chanel for herself. Eric trusted her judgment when he had questions about the society page. Dorothy no longer attended church very often; she still went to the Methodist church if she went at all. That made her somewhat more religious than Stanley, whose attendance was limited to midweek Lenten services in the Lutheran Church with Henry and Renee. Because Stanley worked every Sunday, church was inconvenient.

As they sat in the newsroom one afternoon, Henry brought up the subject of the third political party. Stanley agreed that it was a good idea. But what should they name it?

"Twenty years ago, I would have called it Liberal," said Henry. "But that name has evolved in Europe to mean leftist. We certainly are conservative, but that isn't a really inspiring name."

"Some states already have third parties by that name," said Stanley. "What about Republican?"

"Throughout the South, that name will always be associated with Lincoln," said Henry.

"Well, let's think about the constituency we're seeking. How about Maritime Party?"

"My father said that would remind people of the Shore Party in ancient Athens. We want to attract people from every industry. We should really be looking at wage workers."

"Great Britain has a Labor Party," said Stanley. "Is that what we're looking for?"

"Unfortunately, that party is socialistic. Where do all the pieces of the puzzle converge?"

"They converge on the state. We should name it after the state bird. What about the Pelican Party?"

"That makes more sense than anything else we've said. Stanley, my friend, you did it! You found the perfect name."

One issue facing the Confederacy at this time was the movement for a common currency with the United States. Just after New Year's, Henry came into the newsroom and sat at the long table at his typewriter.

Stanley was already seated on the long side of the table. "Good morning, Henry. What's going on?"

"The common currency issue. It's probably more important than industrialization this year."

"Have you decided yet on the common currency?"

"Yes. I'm going to give it qualified support."

"Holding out for a bimetallic standard?"

"And equal time for our presidents' pictures."

"Wouldn't that involve some retooling?"

"No matter what we do, it would involve retooling."

"Do you think it would bring the two republics closer together?"

"Not now. It would have thirty years ago, but the immigration patterns have built another wall."

"Want some coffee and a doughnut?"

"What kind of doughnuts do they have?"

"Probably only one kind, but I'd still like to know what your preference would be if there were a choice."

"Chocolate," Henry replied. He started typing an editorial he was going to read about Mexico. He began by talking about how the United States never recognized the Empire of Mexico with its Hapsburg imperial family; that was over seventy years ago. They had little choice about it now. Mexico was what it was. "It probably pains them to see the statues of Richard Ewell and Achille Bazaine on the heights of Chapùltepec," he mused aloud.

FRIED OYSTER SANDWICH

"What are you talking about? It sounds as if you mentioned a Confederate general and a French general."

"I was just thinking. Those statues are side by side, commemorating the victory over the Juaristas."

"I remember St. Louis. The statues of Franz Sigel and St. Louis are both in Forest Park."

"Sigel was a Union general. But he was also a Forty-Eighter."

"A what?"

"An immigrant following the failed revolutions of 1848 in Europe. I bet he hates being treated like a crusader. Both statues are equestrian."

"That was ninety years ago."

"You're right. That means we're only ten years away from the centennial."

"Finish your doughnut so I can understand you better."

Henry took a sip of his black chicory coffee. "Ah, 1848. It was a very good year."

"Because of the revolutions?"

"They did take place that year, but the event I want to celebrate is the coronation of Franz Josef II. He became archduke of Austria that year, and soon afterward, he was the emperor of the Dual Monarchy. He reigned longer than any other monarch: sixty-eight years, one more than Louis XIV, if you don't count the Richelieu years."

"Does anybody remember that?"

"When you celebrate a centennial, you don't expect people who remember the original to be on hand."

"Very funny," Stanley replied sarcastically.

Henry grinned. "Eat your doughnut."

"Is that the most important thing you can think to write about?"

"Next week I'm going to write about industrialization."

Stanley went down to his typewriter at the opposite end of the table. "You are resisting the inevitable, Henry."

"By holding out on common currency?"

"No—by resisting industrialization."

"I'm not really resisting it. I was wondering whither common currency might lead."

"I see advantages in bringing the two republics closer together," said Stanley.

"I see dangers," said Henry as he walked over to the teletype machine. "The United States would never go back to the way of choosing presidents prescribed by the Constitution."

"I read that they were even considering eliminating the Electoral College."

"The Confederacy would never descend into that abyss," said Henry. "But the flood of immigrants is changing the nature of the population."

"Anything good on the teletype?"

"Mostly sports right now. I'll save it for you to read."

"Are you guys masking for Mardi Gras?"

"With Flavia around now, we need to stay close to home. Why don't you come to our house?"

"Sounds fine to me."

They met at Henry's house. Eric and Stephanie were there as well. Renee served everyone a glass of Sherry, and then she went to get Flavia while Stanley began the conversation.

"We now have a good idea of the Pelican Party's platform."

"Let me hear it," Stephanie responded.

"We are looking at the maritime interests as our main base. But we are also concerned about industrial laborers."

"They're not all that happy with the Regular Democrats," said Henry.

"We have had meetings with some of the union leaders, but nothing conclusive so far," Stanley continued.

"Have you looked at the salt and sulfur miners?" asked Eric.

"They're on board already," Stanley replied. "No, it's the oil laborers who want minimum wages and more regulations."

"Which present us with a problem?" asked Eric.

"Some of their regulations are common sense," said Henry. "But wages are all tied up with taxes, real estate, interest rates, and the prospect of a common currency with the United States."

Stephanie had another question. "Would common currency give momentum to the industrialization of the Confederacy?"

"And that," Henry continued, "is connected to the question of whether industrialization is a good thing."

"Could that be solved with the regulations?" asked Stephanie. Henry was not surprised at all at his mother's political acumen, but Stanley was taking notice. Stephanie had the time to chair the party.

Renee brought in a plate of hors d'oeuvres: small crab cakes, prosciutto rolls around provolone cheese, and small slices of french bread. Political talk was no longer the focus.

The spring of 1939 brought a new set of considerations. George, the patriarch of the Kaufmann family, was dying. Everyone was calling at the house on Second Street several times a week. Stephanie came every day to sit beside him while the two servants went quietly about their duties. Then Renee was pregnant once more. She was very healthy, small but robust.

George never left his bed, and so on Sunday the family gathered in the dining room to talk about the future.

"We really should keep this house," Eric began. "The taxes aren't that bad, the location is beautiful, and it's near the cemetery where my mother is buried. We can walk easily to St. Charles Ave. to catch the streetcar."

"Would we be able to live here?" asked Linda.

"Is that something you would like, Linda?" asked Henry.

"Of course," the young woman replied.

"And what about the girls?" asked Eric. There were two again: Essie's cousin Susie, had come to work with her. For about a month after George passed, they would be needed to reconfigure the house. Eric and Stephanie had changed their attitude toward the uptown house now that Henry was married and living elsewhere. Besides that, there could be a domino effect here. Henry and Renee could have the house on Clermont Drive, where Henry had grown up. They could sell the house on Johnson Street and open a savings account with the proceeds. That would be the end of the pretty walks in St. Roch Park, but it would mean the children would have the option of attending Capdau Elementary School on Franklin Avenue. Henry's friend, Tommy Farley, had gone to school there.

"Do you suppose your mother would like to hire Essie?" Eric asked Henry.

"Do you think they would work separately?" Henry asked.

"If they had to."

"With three of us living there, it would mean a lot of cleaning," Linda volunteered.

"On the other hand, Henry and Renee will have two children. They might have need of the larger house?"

"The one on Clermont was big enough for Henry and me," Linda replied.

Soon there was an agreement that marked the beginning of the moves two families would make. One complication for Eric and Stephanie would be the distance from their church on Burgundy Street. It had been many years since Eric had attended Zion, although Henry and Linda had been baptized there.

There was no question of the family's right concerning the house. George had written his will years ago and left the house to Eric and Stephanie. They had copies of the will, as did Henry and Renee. Neither was there any question that the family would retain Essie and Susie as long as they could. The servants would certainly want that because the Kaufmanns paid well. The two maids ate in the kitchen, and their menu was the same as what was served in the dining room. After all, this was New Orleans.

George surprised everybody by rallying for a while around Easter, but he took a bad turn around Jubilate. The pastor from Zion came to administer absolution and Holy Communion. George did not last a day after that, and he passed into his celestial dwelling at the age of seventy-nine. His wake was at the house on Second Street, and his funeral was at Zion Church. He was buried next to his beloved Mary in the Washington Avenue Cemetery.

Stanley attended the wake. Renee had hoped he would come with Dorothy, but to everyone's surprise, the young lady he escorted was Elizabeth, Dorothy's partner at the boutique. Renee's matchmaking magic had missed its intended target, but she had made a match nevertheless. Elizabeth had grown up on St. Charles Avenue and was an Episcopalian.

Eric and Stephanie moved into the house on Second Street, where they had talked about the world situation with George back in the days when they were at Tulane. They were a fifteen-minute streetcar ride from Audubon Park, where they had walked along the lagoon. In the same amount of time, they could walk to the Jackson Avenue Ferry, where George had labored. Essie and Susie now worked for them and did not have to move. Linda spent many happy hours walking around her new neighborhood and learning where everything was. A five-minute streetcar ride could bring her to Dorothy's boutique.

A week later, Henry and Renee moved into the house on Clermont Drive. They sold the house on Johnson Street, bought a Dodge, and deposited the rest of the proceeds in a savings account. The neighborhood was almost suburban in its demographics and layout. There were trees everywhere. Henry and Renee each took one of Flavia's hands and walked around. Flavia was not very fast, so the walks took some time. As the year went on, the New Orleans heat and the evening mosquitoes made the walks more difficult. Not even the hotels had air conditioning.

Fried Oyster Sandwich

Vacation time was still two months away, but at least they could open up the camp on weekends. Eric and Stephanie would go there on a Friday evening, and then Henry would pick up Renee after work on Saturday and take the family there for the breeze. It would be a few weeks before the bands would come to Milneburg in the evenings. Still, it was easier to sleep there on the hottest weeks.

In the meantime, Henry had a lot of work to do. The teletype was excited about a development that would link Europe and Mexico. Charles of Hungary, the emperor of the Dual Monarchy since 1916, had no children. As the family looked around for close relatives, they had to cross the Atlantic to find a successor. The imperial dignity appeared to be destined to pass to the Mexican branch of the family. "So Stanley, it looks as though the most probable imperial heir is in our backyard," Henry began.

"You mean the emperor's younger brother?"

"Rodrigo Alejandro. Even though he's middle-aged now."

"Does the Imperial Diet still have to elect him?"

"No; that ended in 1805 with the Holy Roman Empire. The problem is he's a bachelor."

"I would have thought the French might be concerned."

"Remember, Stanley, it's been sixty-nine years since the French were so decisively beaten by the Prussians. Since that time, they haven't had much interest in Mexico. But the imperial family is Austrian, descended from Maximillian, and Belgian on Carlotta's side. Of course they have an interest."

"I see. And from the diminishing pool of royalty, they have to find him a suitable mate."

"That's right. But she has to be the right religion. They can rule out the Protestants, the Orthodox, or any kind of non-Trinitarian. So they have to think Catholic."

"So that doesn't leave too many options, does it?" Stan said.

"You could look at some dispossessed royals, like the Braganzas or the Comte de Paris, or some minor monarchies, like Luxembourg or Monaco."

"Do they have any eligible daughters?"

"None that I can think of.

"What about the Catholic royals?"

"That leaves four families: the Wittelsbachs, the Spanish Bourbons, the House of Savoy, and the Belgian Saxe-Cobrugians. The most promising daughter I can think of is Maddalena, the youngest child of Victor Emmanuel III."

"What would she think of the idea?"

Henry smirked. "Right now, probably not much. She's eleven."

"Does this have to be done very soon?"

"I hope not. Charles isn't sick. He did have a narrow escape seventeen years ago, but he has been well enough lately. I'd say there's a window of opportunity."

"Good. What else is going on?"

"There's the question of common currency. That's becoming more difficult because some states don't like it at all."

"I thought we had that all settled."

"As far as Richmond and Washington are concerned, it is. But it isn't playing in Austin."

"Can we do anything about it?" Stan asked.

"Only what we've been doing: talk about it, advocate it, and show people that it's for the best."

"For how long?"

"God only knows."

Chapter Nine

Henry and Renee's second child was born near the end of July, just as the family was getting ready to go to Milneburg for their vacation. His name was Martin George, and they brought him home on a Friday afternoon. Henry looked at his sleeping son. He was healthy, fairly heavy, and quiet—for now. He was a real mix of Henry and Renee. Renee put little Martin in a bassinet in the living room, and then she fell asleep on the sofa while Henry kept watch. Soon Linda came in with Jacquelyn, whom she had picked up in her way. Henry had a chance to sleep as well, but only for an hour. Stephanie came with Flavia, which meant no one could sleep. Everyone gathered by the large tabletop radio.

Linda tried a playful question with Henry. "How many of Jesus's disciples had names beginning with P?"

"That's a trick question," replied Henry.

"What do you mean?" a puzzled Linda continued.

"In English, there are two that begin with P, but remember that in Greek, one starts with a π, and the other with a ϕ," Henry answered.

"What difference does Greek make?"

Henry started, "If you're talking about the New Testament—and it appears that you are—the standard text is the Greek. So if you're talking about Peter and Philip, they start with the same letter in English, but..."

"That's the right answer," Linda interjected

"What about Paul?" Jacquelyn asked.

"He never really knew Jesus," Linda continued. "He was not an eyewitness of the resurrection or the ascension. He saw a vision."

"Doesn't that count?" asked Stephanie.

"Not if the question is about disciples," Henry replied gently. "Many saints had visions. Only twelve, and one non-saint, actually followed Jesus. Apparently someone named Joseph Barsabbas was one of the faithful who came close to being named among the twelve."

"Was it all men?" asked Stephanie.

"No," her son answered. "Only men could be counted among the twelve, but there were women who followed Jesus from the beginning."

"And children?" asked Linda.

Henry replied, "Well, whenever the Lord needed a child to make a point, one always seemed to be around."

"So, who will be Martin's godfather?"

"We're going to ask Maurice and Jacquelyn to be his godparents," was Henry's firm answer.

Renee stopped him. "Is there any way Dorothy could be his godmother?"

"That is a consideration. But she's Methodist."

"They baptize babies," said Renee.

"And Maurice and Jacquelyn are Catholic," said Stephanie.

"Is that a problem, dear mother-in-law?" asked Henry.

"Don't tell me you don't know dozens of people who have godparents from other churches," said Linda. "After all, Uncle Danny is my godfather. He never goes to church at all."

"I would like Dorothy to do it," said Jacquelyn, "but I think Maurice could stand with her."

"Then it's settled," said Renee. "Dad and Dorothy."

Dorothy lived next door to Maurice and Jackie, and so communicating this would not be a problem.

At the Boutique Bienville, Dorothy and Elizabeth did all the retail work. Their only employee was a janitor, who came on Mondays and Fridays. The girls were the best of friends. The circle was being drawn tighter as Elizabeth and Stanley were getting serious. It was from Dorothy that Stanley learned about the dramatic way Henry and Renee had met. They were doing well enough to hire another retail clerk; Dorothy's sister, Alice, would be offered the job.

Meanwhile, Linda had started dating Gordon, a boy from their church whom she had known since they were teenagers. His grandfather had been a teacher at the church's school. He was an amateur photographer but made his living as a retail clerk selling cameras. He was a few months younger than Linda. His father was a master plumber who liked to drive sports cars. I

On a Thursday evening in late May, Stanley and Elizabeth were double-dating with Gordon and Linda. After parking near St. Ann Street, they walked to the Café du Monde. This was a very popular site, but they were there a little earlier than the main traffic. A waiter in white brought a large pot of coffee and two baskets of beignets to their table.

"If I ever moved from this city, I would miss the smell of the French Quarter," Elizabeth began.

"Kind of a mixture of malt, hops, and pralines," Stanley continued.

"The full moon looks like a honeydew melon," was Gordon's contribution.

"That's because the air is so thick," said Stanley.

Linda led them to a new step. "What amazes me is that we can't really talk about New Orleans without using food similes and references. What do people use when they talk about Chicago, Stanley?"

"The stockyards, the weather, and the Cubs," he replied.

"I think about the railroads," said Linda. "They are what connect the Confederacy with the United States. New Orleans has this in common with Chicago: no trains go through it."

"What do you mean?" asked Gordon.

"Well," said Linda, "If you were going to New York, what railroad would you take?"

"Probably the Southern," he answered.

"Or if you were going to Atlanta?"

"Also the Southern."

"But suppose you were going to San Antonio," Linda countered.

"Then I would have to take the Southern Pacific."

"Or to Memphis?"

"The Illinois Central. It's the only one that works."

"That's what I mean. No one railroad leaves New Orleans going in more than one direction. The same phenomenon is true of Chicago."

"Do trains go through St. Louis?" asked Stanley.

"The Wabash does," Linda replied. "It goes from Detroit to Kansas City. You can leave it going either east or west from St. Louis. My grandfather was from there."

Gordon took another beignet. "I didn't know you had relatives in Missouri," he said. "My great-grandfather was a pastor in Missouri, just as his father had been."

"We should go there together next vacation," said Elizabeth.

"Not go to the camp?" asked Linda.

"We can go there on weekends. I know how much Dorothy likes that."

As Stanley poured himself another cup of coffee, Gordon said, "You've been quiet for a while, Stanley. Are you pondering something?"

"As a matter of fact, I am. Do you think it will ever be all one country again?"

"Henry has thought about that," said Linda. "He says it would have to be a brand-new one. We don't want to become Yankees. They don't want what we have."

"Do you think I'm a Yankee?" asked Stanley.

"You certainly don't talk like one on the radio," Elizabeth answered.

They decided to visit St. Louis in 1940. There would be one more summer at Milneburg.

In mid-June, Henry invited the constituent members of the Pelican Party board to the WOPR newsroom for a meeting. At the head of the table sat Stephanie, who was the party chairman. On her right was Henry and then Stanley, the vice-chairman. To his right was Johnny Labruzzo from the oil refiners' union, who was the secretary. On her left sat Warren McGrory, an officer of the United Fruit Company, and to his left was Marguerite Girod Dumaine, a descendant of the first mayor of New Orleans after the Louisiana Purchase, representing the old families. She owned a large cattle farm in Jefferson Parish, as well as racing stables at Ponchatoula on the north shore.

The first order of business was the party logo. Stanley had a suggestion. "The pelican on the state flag won't do. It's pecking at itself."

"Maybe we need more than one bird," suggested Johnny.

"Let's keep it simple if we can," warned Stephanie.

"Should it be holding objects representing agriculture and industry?" asked Henry.

"Where would the maritime interests be represented?" asked Warren.

"I would like to see it flying," said Mrs. Dumaine.

"That's a great idea," Stephanie agreed. "It would show that we want to move ahead."

"It wouldn't have to be holding anything," said Stanley.

"Once we decide this, we don't want to change it," said Henry.

"Would it be brown?" asked Johnny.

"Brown on top, white on the chest," said Mrs. Dumaine.

"On a purple field," added Henry, "representing Mardi Gras."

"Then I think we have agreement," said Stephanie. "We want a brown pelican on a purple field, flying. Do I hear a motion?"

Warren moved, Johnny seconded, and the logo was adopted. "Next we need to discuss our platform," said Stephanie. "Let's begin by looking at our relationship with the United States. What advantages can we gain from that?"

"We already have considerable commerce between the countries," said Stanley. "We have railroads that connect them. We have ports at which ships from both countries can call. We have unobstructed rivers."

"We could work toward reuniting. But how valuable is our independence?" asked Warren.

"The populations are not equal," said Henry. "The Yankees would be the senior partner."

"But we have the better foreign relations," said Stephanie.

"This is definitely a long-term goal," said Stanley. "And Henry is right about the nature of the union. It would have to be a completely new country."

"That's fine," said Stephanie. "We have more immediate questions to address,"

Johnny lit a cigar and said, "Well, the question of common currency is already on the table. Henry has had a couple of programs about it."

"It appears to be a bone of contention," said Henry. "Within the state, I think it will be accepted, but Texas seems to be very much against it, and probably Oklahoma as well. The committee that worked on it tried to make everybody happy, which is impossible."

"Could we say that our party supports it?" asked his mother.

"Right now, because we're primarily concerned with state issues, I would say so," said Johnny.

"So let's talk about industrialization," said Stephanie.

Stanley was writing down notes, and he paused for a moment. "The industrial wage workers need a party to represent them."

"In the United States, there is a cabinet-level Department of Labor. Would we want something like that?" asked Johnny.

"One step at a time," said Stephanie. "We certainly want to attract those voters. We can do some of that with regulations."

There was general agreement on this subject. There was similar agreement about the bimetallic monetary standard, as well as a fiscal policy based primarily on customs and sales taxes. The last item was infrastructure.

"We want to emphasize the work my husband did to upgrade the levees," said Stephanie. "We should invite him to speak to one of our meetings about it."

"They held in 1927," said Warren.

"Yes, but that did not hit us head-on," said Henry. "We need to keep people aware of that work."

"Should all of our energy be put to state and local issues?" asked Johnny.

"For now, yes. I see some conflict within the Confederacy coming up with that common currency issue. We really can't tell the other states what to do," said Stanley.

"But we do want to run candidates," replied Stephanie. "Our legislators will be serving in Richmond. But you're right for the time being. We are called the Pelican Party for a reason. We're here to serve Louisiana."

Throughout the summer, Renee was busy with both Flavia and Martin still in diapers. Jacquelyn came over most afternoons for a while, and Linda visited on the weekends. Every Monday, Stephanie sent Suzie over to do the wash and ironing. Flavia looked forward to having Suzie in the house. Suzie played with her and bought her a stuffed bear. Both children were very healthy and intelligent. Renee insisted on doing the cooking, but she needed some help getting the ingredients, which Jacquelyn obtained for her. Flavia spoke her first word with Suzie: "Dada."

The following autumn, Henry's last program had ended, and Stanley was minding the teletype. They had been discussing higher education when a report came over the machine saying that the Louisiana legislature would be voting on daylight savings time. "You know, some of the states are really opposed to this," Stanley said. "Especially Kentucky and Tennessee, which span two time zones."

"Alabama used to have that problem too," replied Henry. "The meridian ran through the middle of the town of Anniston. The legislature moved the time zone eastward to the state line. Now it's all in the central zone."

"It was easier for Alabama to do that than Kentucky or Tennessee. They both stretch from the Mississippi River to the Appalachians."

"I think the real divide is between agrarians and industrials," said Henry. "Alabama has become more industrial, so it's bound to opt for

Fried Oyster Sandwich

daylight savings. That's why we have to keep one foot on each side of this issue."

Stanley poured himself a glass of water. As he returned to his seat, he asked Henry, "What is it that you find so valuable in classical education?"

Henry wasn't quite ready for that question, so he did what any experienced interviewer would do: he shifted the discussion to something he knew a lot about. "Stanley, can you name the seven liberal arts?"

"I don't even know why they call them that," Stanley replied.

"Liberal arts as opposed to servile arts. Those that liberate the person rather than locking him into some kind of service."

"There are seven of these?"

"Yes. First there are the arts of the Trivium—namely grammar, logic, and rhetoric. Then there are the four arts of the Quadrivium, which are geometry, mathematics, music, and astronomy. And no, I didn't study all seven, at least not formally. You must have had something like that."

"At Northwestern we took courses in English, science, at least one other language, and what they called social science. The language I studied was French."

"That didn't take four years."

"Of course not. I had a major and a minor, just as you did. That didn't leave time for much philosophy."

"I minored in philosophy, so I had to make time for it. I majored in Latin and Greek, and I elected to take the history courses I loved so much, as well as German."

"What about French and Spanish?"

"My parents spoke French. Besides, I had Spanish and French in high school. Greek came in handy with the philosophy, because you begin with the ancients. I also studied Descartes and Hume, and I had one course on Hegel. I passed over the French *philosophes*. My first impression of them made me angry."

"Northwestern's main aim was to enable us to pursue a career."

Henry went to get a cup of coffee, and he returned ready to answer Stanley's original question. "A classical university's main aim is to make every student capable of critical thought. Not a day goes by when we do not apply that ability."

"Are you making a good living with it?"

"I make a good living because I'm interested in my work and put some effort into it. Having character is so important, because I'm dealing in informing the public."

The teletype interrupted them. The following year would be a presidential election. Huey Long had announced that he was running again. Certainly Muldoon's party would field a candidate. "Tomorrow, could you hang around until I get off? I have something special to talk to you about."

"Of course, Stanley. Shall we get a drink at Danny's Tavern?"

"Right after work. That's fine."

The two friends went to the tavern together the next afternoon. They sat at a booth and ordered shots—scotch for Stanley, Irish for Henry. Stanley lit a cigarette as Henry pushed the ash tray in his direction. After a long draught on the smoke, Stanley said, "Elizabeth and I are getting married."

"Well, congratulations to you two. I can't say it's a big surprise."

Fried Oyster Sandwich

"Thanks. How would you like to be the best man?"

"It would be an honor. Do you have a date set?"

"It isn't final yet. Probably around Mardi Gras."

"Are you getting a king cake with a little bride and groom on it?"

"I knew that was coming," said Stanley.

The year 1940 began with excitement. It was a presidential election year, and there was tension in the republic over the common currency with the United States. In February, Stanley and Elizabeth were married in Trinity Church Episcopal on St. Charles Ave. They moved into a house on Prytania Street. Essie stayed away from the wedding because of her religion, but attended the reception.

In March, the Progressive Party caucus had nominated J. Strom Thurmond of South Carolina for president, much to Muldoon's displeasure. Henry and Stanley were happy with the choice. Their own Pelican Party did not nominate a candidate, saving their energy and resources for the gubernatorial election of 1941. They did nominate Robert Fredricks, whom Johnny Labruzzo had introduced, for the position of Orleans Parish manager. He finished second in a five-way race. Henry had no trouble getting guests to interview; scheduling programming was easy when people came to him. In June he even had the Mexican ambassador on his program. The ambassador invited him to visit Chapúltepec.

Christmas was rather warm that year, about sixty degrees. Three-year-old Flavia danced around the tree, one-year-old Martin scooted around in a walker. Eric and Stephanie, Maurice and Jacquelyn, Henry and Renee, Gordon and Linda, Essie and Suzie, and the unescorted Dorothy and Elizabeth (Stanley was on the air) celebrated, played with the children, and relaxed as they digested their Christmas dinner. After about an hour, Stephanie, Jackie, Renee, and Dorothy moved to the kitchen, where they tackled the small mountain of dishes that needed cleaning. They all talked at the same time yet somehow understood each other. It had taken several years of practice, but by then they were used to it. That left the men in the living room with Linda, Elizabeth, Essie, Suzie, and the children. Essie and Suzie were not supposed to work that day; they were guests. They played with Flavia and Martin, and the others gathered around the radio.

Eric was the patriarch of the family now. He sat in the easy chair next to the mantelpiece in the living room. "So do we agree that President Thurmond will be good for the country?" he began.

Linda finally gave him an answer. "Dad, he has his work cut out for him. The international situation is anything but stable."

"Look at Europe," said Gordon. "Italy seems ripe for some kind of change."

"They have a constitutional monarchy, don't they?" said Maurice.

"Only theoretically," said Henry. "All Europe recognizes Victor Emmanuel as the king, but he directly rules only Savoy and Sardinia. In Venice and Tuscany, he can approve or disapprove what their parliaments enact, but he has no authority to initiate legislation. In Rome, he is like a president who rules together with the senate. The Roman senate also has authority over the judicial system, the monetary system, and foreign policy for the whole country. He is the protector of the Vatican, a position formerly held by the French. In other parts of Italy, Lombardy, Naples, and Sicily, the only sign of his reign is his picture on the money."

"But nobody is challenging him in those provinces?" asked Elizabeth.

"There would be nothing to gain by it," Henry replied. "They have local order and low taxes. None of them seem to be unhappy."

"Does the king live in Rome?" asked Maurice.

"He has a residence there in the Palazzo Farnese," said Eric. "But he also has homes in Turin and Florence. He is still the hereditary Duke of Savoy."

"Wait a minute what's this?" Henry said. The music program on the radio had ended, and after a commercial, the news had come on.

"Sounds like there's trouble in Manchuria," said Gordon.

"A three-way trouble," said Eric. "Manchuria was never happy under Japanese rule. Now other countries are trying to do something about it."

"Who can take on Japan?" asked Gordon.

"Sounds like it's all local," said Henry. "The Kuomintang have partisans in Manchuria, even though they haven't been very active lately. Now it appears the Soviets have some as well, and they have moved troops near the border."

"Didn't Stalin say he couldn't turn it into a socialist republic because it had never been a bourgeois one?" asked Eric.

"He did," Henry answered, "but seven years of Japanese conquest could substitute for that."

"What does all that have to do with us?" asked Elizabeth.

"It's impossible to tell now. We are not a Pacific power, but our neighbors are. Both the United States and Mexico are on the Pacific. The Yankees have air service from San Francisco to Shanghai on the China Clipper, an amphibious passenger route," said Henry.

"Isn't that too long a flight?" asked Linda.

"They stop at Oahu, Wake, and Guam," Eric replied.

"It looks as though Stanley and I are not going to be devoting much time to local politics, at least not on the air," said Henry.

At home, Henry and Renee found time for a puppy. Dorothy's parents had a pair of dogs, a Labrador and a collie. The resulting puppies were rather curious. There were six of them, five of which the Petersons were giving away. Renee picked out a little tan female and named it Patachou, meaning something like "Brussels sprout." When she was weaned, they brought her to the house on Clermont Drive. At first the dog slept on a small pillow in Henry and Renee's room. As she grew, they put down a soft rug for her to sleep on. Flavia and Martin were happy with the puppy. They didn't yet appreciate how fortunate they were to have the privilege of growing up with a pet in the house.

At WOPR, there were many news items to discuss. Henry's father was trotting out his levee project again because the spring of 1941 was rather wet. Henry had him as a guest on his morning interview show. "So, Dad, do you think the city needs to put more emphasis on the river levees?"

"All the levees—the river, the lake, and all the canals. The ones we have serve us well in ordinary weather, but a hurricane could overwhelm them."

"As you know, this is a gubernatorial year. Do you think the levees should be a political issue?" Henry asked.

"I understand the Pelican Party has a candidate for the primary."

"We do. We are running Joseph Wagner, a New Orleans lawyer. And Warren McGrory will be our candidate for Lieutenant Governor."

Eric said, "Besides the levees, I want to warn people about living on the batture. I know how pleasant it can be. When your mother and I were in college, we used to go walking there, near Audubon Park. But in the 1937 storm, a few of the houses were swept away.

Few things in this world are as powerful as the Mississippi when it's out of control."

"You have published editorials about that, right?"

"Yes, of course. But we need to keep this on everyone's mind, so we need to make sure your medium is involved as well."

"The canals all connect with the lake, don't they?" Henry asked.

"Yes. The London Avenue, Orleans Avenue, New Basin, and Seventeenth Street canals all flow into Lake Pontchartrain. We might as well count Bayou St. John too. Putting locks there was a good idea, but it needs better levees."

There was a commercial break. During the break, the country singer Eddie Arnold came into the studio. Henry introduced him to Eric. "Eddie is going to be singing live on the air here this weekend," said Henry. "He promised to make an appeal about the levees."

"Thank you so much, Mr. Arnold," said Eric. "I have been working on this since 1915, two years after Henry was born. There has been opposition."

"My dad served on a mayor's commission to study the problem years ago," added Henry. "He does a good job publicizing it in the Picayune."

When the commercial ended, the engineer made a sign to Henry that he was about to turn the studio mike back on. Eric said his good-byes, and Henry brought the singer to the mike.

At Easter, Henry and Renee brought the children to the house on Second Street. Martin had spoken his first words while they were visiting. Eric had witnessed that event. The children had hunted for Easter eggs in the fenced-in yard. Essie was getting arthritis in her ankles, and she could not keep up with the children—which were going to increase. By May, both Renee and Elizabeth were expecting. They were due at about the time the elections would be held, in which the Pelican Party would play a role. This was a gubernatorial year.

That week Henry had his mother as a guest. She would be interviewing some gubernatorial candidates. While they were in the newsroom, the teletype began chattering. Henry took the copy over to the long table and showed it to Stephanie.

"That could be really bad news," said Stephanie. "Texas has threatened to secede over the common currency. They really are against it."

"Could somebody, someday, tell me what is so wrong with common currency?" asked Henry.

"As a native of Oklahoma, I remember growing up with multiple currencies. In Arkansas and Texas, we used Confederate. In Missouri and Kansas, we used US. And in Tulsa we had all of them. We managed all right, but it would have been convenient to have had it all the same."

"But both the Confederacy and the United States have bent over backward this time. They have made all sorts of concessions. After all that hard work, what could make Texas so intransigent?"

"Too bad we don't have any Texans here to ask," said Stephanie.

"We accepted their denominations and format. They accepted our bimetallic standard and heroes' pictures. Have you read anything about the Texas point of view?"

"Not very much. But one article I read believed this would be a stepping stone to bringing the Confederacy back into the Union. Do you think that's a valid objection?"

"No," said Henry. "Getting together with them would be advantageous, but not as their country. We would want a new one"

"The Pelican Party has that as part of its platform," Stephanie replied. "Incidentally, when Eddie Arnold was here, I approached him about giving a benefit concert for the Pelican Party in August."

"Is that fear the only reason?" asked Henry.

"If so, then the whole state is assuming a lot. But what do we do about it?"

"It is the Lone Star State."

"Not very original. They got that name, and that flag, from West Florida."

"And they were never part of West Florida. But to answer your question, I would say pray hard. And if we do get to talk to any Texans, try to show them some sense."

"Could you schedule any face-to-face debates?"

"Good suggestion, Mom. I'll try to get one of their senators on the air."

Henry saw this year as a crossroads for Louisiana, but hardly anybody knew why. He programmed candidates for the other parties and had his mother interview them; she knew the hard questions that had to be asked. But the election proved Henry right. The Progressive Party and Regular Democrats had lost their duopoly. Earl Long, the standard-bearer of the Regular Democrats, was elected governor, but the Pelican Party came in second. Muldoon finished a distant third.

Texas dropped its demands over the common currency. Apparently, the whole misunderstanding was about Texan identity. When the Confederate Athletic Association told them that if they seceded, their football teams couldn't play in the accustomed conference, Texas backed down.

LLOYD E. GROSS

December also saw two new babies make their appearance in the world. Elizabeth and Renee both had little girls, first Lisa Kozar in late November, and then Denise Kaufmann in early December. Henry and Renee were Lisa's godparents, and Stanley and Elizabeth were Denise's. Jacquelyn made the babies' footprints on index cards with a stamp pad. She gave a copy to Renee, who had them framed and put up on the wall in the children's room. When the two-year-old Martin saw the display, he said, "Mommy, are those feet?"

"Yes," Renee replied, "Denise's and Lisa's."

"Who is Lisa?" the toddler asked innocently.

Part IV

Martin and Lisa

Chapter Ten

MARTIN WAS EIGHT YEARS OLD in late September 1947. There was no school today, even though it was a Wednesday. When he looked outside the living room window, he saw why. The trees were blowing this way and that much harder than he had ever seen. It was starting to rain, as hard as a midsummer thunderstorm.

"Flavia, what's happening?"

"I really don't know," Flavia said as she ran into the room, looking puzzled. "It's not like anything that happened here."

If the children thought the weather would slacken, they were mistaken. They watched it for more than fifteen minutes as conditions deteriorated. Henry and Renee came in. The children didn't understand why their father had not gone to work.

"I called the Kozars," said Henry. "High wind and rain there. Stanley thinks the Garden District might have some flooding."

"Where's Denise?" asked Renee.

"Still in the bedroom," Flavia replied. Lightning shone briefly through the window, followed by a very loud clap of thunder.

"Is anybody at the station?" asked Renee.

"Stanley said Lawrence stayed all night. I don't think we're on the air, though." He turned on the radio, but the static drowned out all the stations. Denise had been awakened by the thunder and was afraid. Henry went to the bedroom, picked her up in his arms, and carried her into the living room, where the rest of the family waited.

"It's a hurricane, Denise," said Flavia. "It's a really bad storm with winds over seventy-five miles an hour, and it's getting worse."

"How long will it last?" asked Martin.

"That depends on how much of it hits us," Henry replied. "According to the teletype last night, the eye is coming over the city. It covers a large area. They sometimes change direction, taking a curvy path."

Renee knew there was nothing they could do about it. "Let's go to the kitchen for breakfast."

After they finished their breakfast, they went back into the living room. They tried to listen to the radio, but the static was worse, and then the power went out. Pieces of brick walls were becoming dangerous projectiles.

"The refrigerator won't work until the power comes back on, so we'll eat what's in there until it does," Renee advised them.

"Does the phone work?"

"Yes, Martin, as long as that cable doesn't blow down."

"Then let's call Grandma Stephanie."

Henry made the call. Everybody was well at the house on Second Street, as well as on Claiborne Avenue. Martin went back to the living room window. Denise was too afraid to look. Flavia cuddled her but was ill at ease herself. Martin watched as the wind blew down the chimney from the house across the street. The rain was as hard as it had been all day, but the water was draining away rather well.

"All right," said Henry. "Why are we all still in our pajamas? I realize no one is coming, but I would be more comfortable dressed."

"I wish Lisa were here," said Denise.

Renee went over to her youngest child. "I thought we could try dressing different ways," she said, "and perhaps try new hairdos."

"And several colors of nail polish," Flavia contributed.

Meanwhile, Stanley and Elizabeth were in their new house on Prytania Street, a little south of St. Charles Avenue, a short distance from Boutique Bienville. This was a low-lying area of the city. Lisa woke up to lightning and thunder, and she ran into her parents' bedroom. They were not there, so she began to cry.

Elizabeth heard Lisa crying, and she called to her. "We're in the kitchen, sweetheart."

Lisa ran down the steps, with thunder providing the mood music. Stanley and Elizabeth were checking over their food supply, knowing it would not be long before the power went out. "Mommy, Daddy, what's happening?" Lisa asked.

"It's a hurricane, sweetheart," said Stanley. "A bad, bad storm with lots of wind and rain. It lasts all day."

They tried the radio but had the same static problem as Henry and Renee. Then they talked to Henry and Renee on the telephone. The rain hadn't become a big problem yet, but the wind was frightening. "Are you hungry, Lisa? We can make breakfast."

For seven hours, the storm continued. The eye did not hit New Orleans and glanced by to the west. The wind began to die down. Stanley opened the window. It was still raining, but not as hard as before. There was some flooding in the street, enough to have a current pulling the water southward toward the river, but only about a foot deep. "Take a look upstairs, Liz," he called over. "Check the rooms."

Elizabeth went upstairs. She found that water was leaking into their bedroom from the ceiling. "Stanley, something must have happened to the roof. We have a leak."

"Where?"

"In the bedroom, in the corner by the window."

"How bad is it?"

"We can catch it in the big bucket, but we'll have to empty it every couple of hours."

"Well, we can't do anything about it now. We'll have to get through the night as best we can."

"Do you think the rain will stop?"

"Let's try the radio again. Maybe someone is on the air."

There was still a lot of static, but Stanley found one station where he could decipher what the announcer was saying. He listened for half an hour and then heard a weather report. "Liz, Lisa, good news. The levees held. There won't be a major flood."

"What about the rain?"

"It should be stopping around eleven this evening."

By morning, the phone was working again. Elizabeth called Henry and Renee. They invited the Kozar family to stay with them in Edgewood until their roof was repaired. By midafternoon, Stanley and

Fried Oyster Sandwich

Elizabeth has put their house in the best order they could, and they packed a week's worth of clothes for themselves and Lisa. The streets were passable again for cars, but not many people were about. The rain had stopped, and the sun came out.

Flavia answered the doorbell when the company arrived. Martin and Denise ran into the living room to greet them. Henry had gone to work, but Renee was more than capable of extending the Kaufmann hospitality.

"We are so glad to have you," she began. Before she could finish, Elizabeth interrupted her.

"What would we ever do without you?"

"You aren't without us, Mrs. Kozar," said Flavia. "We're going to have a fun week."

"No school until next Thursday," said Martin.

"We brought sleeping bags. We can stay in the living room," said Stanley.

"Can I stay with Lisa?" asked Denise.

Renee gave her consent with a wink of her eye. The children shared the room that had been Henry's. The one that had been Linda's was a sewing room, in which there was a day bed. When Linda was single, she had stayed over there some weekends. Now, she and Gordon were married and living on Almonaster Avenue, near North Claiborne, not far from the Gautiers' old house.

Martin and Flavia had their difficult moments sharing a bedroom, not just with each other but Denise as well. Martin loved his sisters but did not necessarily enjoy their company, at least not all the time. He had met Lisa several times because the families did things together.

"Do you play rummy, Lisa?" he asked.

"What's that?"

"A card game. Flavia, Denise, and I play it. We'll be glad to teach you."

Lisa and Denise were six years old. The older children understood that they would have to help the two little girls with things.

Renee set up a card table in the kitchen. "You children can eat in here. The dining room is for the adults."

At suppertime, Henry was back home. Martin watched as Flavia set the table in the kitchen, and Renee set the dining room. He sat across from Flavia, each having a younger child to his side. Denise was having trouble cutting her food.

"Here, let me help you," said Flavia.

Martin took his cue from his sister. "Would you like me to cut yours, Lisa?"

"Yes, thank you."

"It's no trouble. I'm glad you're here. Let me know what you like."

In the dining room, the talk was about Boutique Bienville. Elizabeth began. "We had a lot of damage at the shop. Water got in."

"Will it take long to repair it?" asked Renee.

"I don't know yet. Dorothy said she's going in every afternoon. She has to get everything organized again. I think workmen are coming in."

"Did you lose any of the clothes?"

"Probably not much. How is the station?"

"No damage at all," Henry replied. "We're on the fourth floor of the Jung. Stanley and I will work our normal hours. I think Linda can come in as usual."

Stanley then had another idea. "Is Tulane Stadium all right? Will the game be played Saturday?"

"I'll check in the morning," said Henry.

Flavia overheard this part. "Are we going to the game, Dad?"

"Do you want to?" he asked.

"Yes, yes, yes!" was the high-pitched response of the older children.

Stanley would have to be at the station at that time, but Henry could easily take all four of the children. Flavia and Martin had been to a game with Renee the previous year, but this would be completely new to Denise and Lisa.

"We have to be sure the stadium isn't badly damaged," Henry stated, not wanting to incite false hopes.

He needn't have worried. Tulane Stadium was in good shape. When Saturday arrived, Henry brought all four children to seats high up on the west side. The visiting team was from the University of Georgia. During halftime, Henry took the children to the WOPR booth. The Bulldogs beat the Wave 14–6.

Linda came over on Sunday, and she, Henry, and Stanley had a meeting about the station. Henry was the executive manager, Stanley was the advertising manager, and Linda was the assistant manager.

"Look what your Uncle Gordon bought you, Martin," she said as she took out a small flag: the Stars and Bars, the official icon of the Confederacy. The children decided to have a parade, but Flavia stayed out because she thought she was too old for such things. She turned on the tabletop radio in the living room because a classical music program was coming on.

Meanwhile, the adults had their meeting. "We are at the point when the three of us can all have the weekends off," Linda began.

"It's true," said Stanley. "We have sufficient staff to cover it all. Especially during football season, when we have the broadcast."

"Can you deal with all the advertisers in five days?" Henry asked.

"I'm certainly willing to try."

"Does Gordon have the weekends off?"

"Not always, but often enough. We don't have kids but are always glad to stay with yours."

"What about the news?" asked Stanley.

"I think the war in Asia is over," Henry replied. "The Japanese, the Chinese, and the Soviets are all exhausted. I thought the Yankees might get involved, especially at the time when the Japanese were pushing the Chinese out of Manchuria. Then the Soviets attacked from the other direction. Everything changed."

"They did move an army into the Philippines," Stanley remarked.

"That was because Japan sent a fleet into the South China Sea."

"What a diplomatic blunder that turned out to be!" Linda exclaimed.

"I'll say. Australia mobilized. The Dutch sent an army to Java. Yet none of that had any impact on Manchuria."

"But they're all going home now, aren't they?" Linda asked.

Fried Oyster Sandwich

Henry got up to get a cup of coffee. "Want any?" he asked.

"I do," said his sister.

Henry took his seat again and explained. "We can thank the French for that."

"It was their negotiating that brought about peace," said Stanley.

"They agreed to sell the Japanese oil. They made a treaty that required Japan to leave the South China Sea, but to have use of the base at Camranh Bay. Freighters and tankers could call there at will, but only nine warships—no battleships."

"What about the Chinese and the Soviets?"

"They were there too. They allowed the Japanese to keep the port of Darien on the Manchurian mainland. Japan could withdraw without losing face. And the Chinese and Soviets took out their own armies while supplying partisans in Manchuria."

"So all is settled?" asked Linda.

"It did stir up the Mexicans a bit. They can depend on us to protect the Caribbean coast, but the Pacific is another matter. Emperor Francisco Jose is recruiting a navy. He has plans to build a major base at Puerto Vallarta."

"Why did Manchuria bother Mexico?" Martin asked. Henry didn't realize that Martin was listening. This question made everybody look at the eight-year-old.

"I'm glad you asked, son," said Henry. "Japan is the greatest maritime power in the world, with the United States a close second."

"And we're a minor maritime nation," said Stanley. "We trade mostly with the United States and Latin America."

"So though we don't have to worry about what's in the Pacific ocean, the Mexicans do," Henry continued.

The children would have to return to school on Thursday. Even though the workmen weren't quite finished, the Kozar family was making ready to return home. They left on Tuesday afternoon. Flavia helped Renee clean up after the visit. She, Martin, and Denise would go to Pierre A. Capdau School. Lisa would be going uptown.

Lawrence Kraemer was WOPR's new news editor. He was a native of the Crescent City who had grown up in a German neighborhood near the river, below Elysian Fields Avenue. He was a Methodist who attended an old German church on North Rampart Street, around the corner from where the city's only remaining German language newspaper was printed. He was two years older than Gordon, whom he had met during the two years he'd attended the Lutheran school on Burgundy Street. Lawrence was a bachelor and spent a lot of time in the French Quarter. He also spoke German well.

On a day in late September, he walked into the newsroom. He sat down on the side away from the teletype, close to Henry. He had a request. "I would like to cover the imperial wedding in Turin. How does that go with you?"

"What wedding?" Stanley asked from the other end of the table.

"He means Don Rodrigo's," Henry replied.

"Why all the way to Italy?"

Lawrence answered. "The bride's native city is Turin, the capital of Savoy. I'm talking about Princess Maddalena. Her father is King Victor Emmanuel III."

As a matter of fact, she was his third child and only daughter. His oldest son, Raimondo, had been killed in a car racing accident in Monte

Carlo. His younger son, Vitale, was now his heir. As for Don Rodrigo, he was the brother of the emperor of Mexico, Francisco Jose.

"Isn't it odd how these things come about?" asked Henry. "When our country helped the French rescue the Mexican monarchy, who would have thought that the real benefit would be to the Austrian Hapsburgs?"

"Now they're down to their last heir," said Lawrence. "Charles of Hungary had no children. So now this Mexican in late middle age is marrying a twenty-year-old princess."

"He's almost fifty, isn't he?" asked Stanley.

"Born in 1898," Lawrence replied. "Now Secretary Kaplan will be attending all the imperial events. He knows I speak German, so he wants me to accompany him."

Lawrence was talking about Isaac Kaplan, a New Orleans merchant and the third generation of his family to own a large department store on Canal Street. He was very active in the Progressive Party, which was his ladder to becoming secretary of state.

"He's always a welcome guest on the station," said Henry. "His family was always civic-minded. His grandfather was an immigrant from Hungary."

"That's how he learned to speak Magyar," said Lawrence. "I know I could help him with the German."

"In Turin?" asked Stanley.

"Remember, I said 'all the imperial events.' The wedding is just the beginning. From there, it's on to Vienna, where the couple will be invested with their titles as archduke and archduchess. That's where the German comes in. Then on to Budapest, where they will be invested as crown prince and princess."

"How long would you be gone?" Henry asked.

"Three weeks."

Linda entered the room. "What's going on, guys?"

"We were talking about the imperial wedding," said her brother. "Why don't you take a look at the teletype?"

"Just a minute. There's something coming through about the money conference in Richmond. Apparently there's been some agreement."

"Really?" asked Henry.

"They're talking about who's there—legislators and treasury secretaries from the United States and the Confederate States. They agreed that each republic would have its own central bank."

"What about the bimetallic standard?"

"Each would have its own specie reserves."

"Of what metal?"

"Patience, brother. Here we go ... yes they agreed on a bimetallic standard."

"Hallelujah!"

"It will be the general pattern of the US dollar, but the pictures would include some historic Confederate personalities."

"This is a big step toward unity," said Stanley.

"I've heard talk about that," said Linda. "Some are predicting a brand-new North American nation, perhaps including Canada as well."

This sort of talk was irresistible to politicians, who tended to ignore centrifugal forces.

"Within a year, New Orleans will have broadcast television," Linda continued.

"Are you still reading the teletype?" asked Lawrence.

"Hey, video technicians will be moving here."

"I also understand that two of our competitors will be branching into television broadcasting. We have no plans to do that, at least not in 1948. But I see a societal crossroads up ahead."

The following week, Henry and Stanley were at the long table in the newsroom discussing the upcoming elections. Henry said "The Pelicans need to hang onto their plurality in the Louisiana House of Representatives. We mustn't underestimate the blue-collar workers."

"We've got 40 percent. The Progressives and Regular Democrats each have 30 percent."

"Do you see a realignment?"

Just then, Lawrence entered the room; he would be on in the middle of the day, broadcasting in about half an hour. He sat in the middle of the table. "What do you think of the state political parties that are arising all over the Confederacy?" He was referring to the Alamo Party in Texas, the Volunteer Party in Tennessee, and the Cavalier Party in Virginia. These all shared their states' nicknames.

Henry answered. "I expect to see them in the states where the women vote: North Carolina, Florida, Arkansas."

"Since you mention North Carolina," said Stanley, "they have a Conservative Party. It was active in the gubernatorial election."

"Industrialization is well underway there."

"That's right," Lawrence affirmed. "But just because women vote doesn't mean they have anybody like your mother, Henry."

"Did you know she was from Oklahoma?"

"She ought to run for the senate."

"She's a grandmother," Henry replied.

Lawrence turned to Stanley. "Did the Conservative Party have any success?"

Before he could answer, the teletype began chattering. Henry went over to retrieve the copy. "Hang onto your belts," he proclaimed. "The Confederate Congress has passed a tariff. It was a fairly close vote."

"It would have to be," said Stanley. "That has been a bone of contention since the unpleasantness of the nineteenth century. Lincoln's insistence upon it alienated the more agricultural states."

"Time has changed the Confederacy," said Lawrence. "We're more divided on the question than we were eighty-seven years ago."

"Look at Virginia, North Carolina, and Alabama. They're more industrial than agricultural," said Henry.

"Where do we fit in?" asked Stanley.

"A rather unique position," said Henry. "Rather like Kentucky. They lead the country in river boat production; we lead in ship production. We both have industry, but it's related to agriculture and tobacco for them, and sugar, brewing, and canning for us."

"The merchants and bankers will definitely like it," said Lawrence.

"Texas and Oklahoma would be strongly opposed," said Henry. "Also, South Carolina and Mississippi."

"Well, I'm glad we have it," said Stanley. "Those electrical power projects are starting to bring benefits." He was referring to dams along the Tennessee and Cumberland Rivers, which had been built under the presidency of Harry Byrd.

"And consider the textile industry," said Henry. "The upper Chattahoochee Valley is alive with it. In North Carolina they are second only to tobacco."

"We have the Industrial Canal," added Lawrence. "And consider the new shipyards at Pensacola and Pascagoula."

The teletype was still for a while. Stanley asked, "What will the oil companies think?"

"It won't change things much for them," Henry answered. "They don't import very much."

"The farmers won't like it," said Lawrence. "That's why the Progressive Party wants to fight it."

"Texas would be divided," said Stanley. "The rice growers like the tariff; the ranchers and cotton people do not. I think the rice growers are part of the Alamo Party."

"What will the Mexicans think?" asked Lawrence.

"Let's wait until we read exactly what they passed. I heard somewhere that Mexico might be exempt from the tariff."

"As for the United States," Henry injected, "they have tariffs of their own with which we can now compete."

Lawrence got a cup of coffee. He looked at the pot for a while and then said, "Coffee could be a problem. We import all of it from South America. You know how New Orleanians love coffee."

"Actually, we'll be in the middle," said Henry, "because the Yankees buy it from us."

"It's a wash, like automobiles. We buy nearly all of them from the United States, but the gasoline nearly all comes from here," said Stanley. "I don't see this as an issue for the Pelican Party at all." This was met with general agreement.

In 1948, it was a presidential year. The Democratic Party held its general caucus in Richmond in March; the Conservative Party had a caucus in Vicksburg a week later. Linda approached her brother to see whether he would consider running as a Pelican. Henry didn't want to speak for the party. He thought his mother would be a better candidate, but she had gone to the Conservative Party caucus.

Henry and his sister were at the newsroom table when Johnny Labruzzo came calling. "Any news about the caucuses?" he asked.

Linda was by the teletype machine. "The Democrats have nominated a Kentuckian, Albert Benjamin Chandler."

"Happy Chandler?" asked Johnny.

"The same," said Henry. "Stanley and my mother are meeting with the Conservatives now. They'll call when they have news."

"And I understand the Progressives are thinking about a Texan. Somebody I've never heard of," said Linda.

"His name in Lyndon Johnson," said Henry. "Flavia is in the fifth grade now. I really would like to bring her here one day. She needs to be acquainted with the local political scene."

Johnny volunteered to take her to a union meeting. "And you should taste her Cajun cooking," said Linda.

At home that evening, Henry brought up the subject of family vacations. Flavia was in the fifth grade now, so Henry asked her first.

"I like going down the river," she replied. "I like to look at the ships that are waiting for births in New Orleans. And I love those ferries, especially the one from Bellechase to Braithwaite."

"You have such a good memory, Flavia," said Renee. "I remember the essay you wrote about the ships sitting at anchor by the Chalmette Monument."

"I remember her sonnet about the orange groves going down to the river from the plantation houses," said Henry. "My Flavia thinks in pentameters."

"It really isn't very hard to do," said Martin. "The camp at Milneburg would get my vote."

"All right, enough iambic banter," said Renee. "Your father probably wants to go farther away this year."

"Could we go with Grandma Jackie?" asked Denise.

"They take me down the river," said Flavia.

"I want to acquaint you all with more historical sites. We could go to Alabama to visit the William Faulkner Dam."

"What's that?" asked Martin.

"It's a huge dam on the Tennessee River, built in 1924, two years before your mother and I met at Milneburg. You can ride in a boat into the lock and be lifted up to the upper river or down to the lower river. It also makes electricity."

"It completely changed the river's role in the economy," said Renee. "It bypasses Muscle Shoals, so you can navigate the river from Knoxville to Paducah."

"How long would it take?" asked Martin.

"I figure six days," said Henry. "We're going by car, you see. It takes a day and a half to go, the same to return. We'd have two days there, and one just in case. We might be back in five."

"Where would we stay?" asked Flavia.

"In Florence," said Henry.

"So we would have time to spend at the camp too," said Martin.

"And time for the girls and me to practice cooking," said Renee.

"She makes great fillo dough," said Henry.

"When Grandma Jackie comes, they make those great Cajun dishes," said Denise.

Flavia was also close to Grandma Stephanie. She liked to hear the stories of her great-grandfather, who'd captained the Jackson Avenue ferry. She enjoyed the streetcar ride there. As for the Gautier grandparents, they had taken her to New Iberia when she was seven. She still remembered the road, especially the bridges they'd crossed on the way.

All of the children were intelligent and observant. There was never a want of babysitters. Martin had a special relationship with his Aunt Linda. She and Gordon had a new hobby: renting aircraft by the hour and flying them down at Joy Airport in Chalmette. They began by renting a two-seater, and one would fly while the other rode as a passenger. Soon they graduated to single-seat planes, chasing each other around the city. When Martin was visiting them, they took him along; one would rent a two-seater to take Martin up. This was Linda's idea. She had always been impressed by her Uncle Danny, a commercial pilot who lived in Dallas. Martin was also fascinated by his great-uncle.

The youngest, Denise, tended to prefer Stanley and Elizabeth because they had Lisa, who was her age. Henry, Renee, Gordon, and Linda joined the Kozars in a trio of couples that did many things together. That meant that Lisa spent a great deal of time with the Kaufmann children. The camp at Milneburg was large enough to accommodate all of them. The older generation was also at the camp. Eric was the one who'd bought it. The children talked to one another about all these experiences.

Flavia wanted to fly with her aunt, so Henry and Renee worked out a schedule, giving Martin more time with his mother's parents and Flavia more time with Gordon and Linda. Martin learned from Jackie the story of how his parents had met in 1926. He had never heard it before because Henry was self-conscious about it, but Martin thought it was truly romantic.

"So, Grandma Jackie, divine Providence arranged for me to be part of your family."

"That's right, Martin. And your sisters as well."

"Did Flavia know this? She never mentioned it to me."

"Probably not. Your father used to get embarrassed when your mother told that story. I don't think he does any longer."

"What's to be embarrassed about? He was a hero."

"I think it was the way your mother told the story," said Jackie.

"Ah, yes," said Martin. "I can well imagine that."

The next time Martin saw Flavia, he told her what his grandmother had told him. Flavia checked it with Renee and was impressed by her version of it. As for Martin, the next time he was with Gordon and Linda, he asked his aunt about it. Not only did they verify every word, but Linda even added the detail about lending Renee her sandals that afternoon, which were big on her even though she was two years older.

Elizabeth took Denise and Lisa to the Boutique Bienville whenever they had a Saturday together. They learned the story of Henry and Renee from Dorothy, who knew it better than anybody. Dorothy found the continuity of generations at the camp at Milneburg very comforting. She told the girls about the simulated rescues she used to play with Henry and Renee. They thought about doing something similar that would involve Martin. Flavia always wanted to be with adults, so Martin was prevailed upon to take care of the little girls. Martin really liked Dorothy. He knew nothing about women's clothing, but Dorothy could tell him so much about his parents.

Martin also cherished the time he spent with Grandpa Eric. Every year on a holiday, Grandpa Eric would take him to the newspaper office, where Martin could see the teletypes at work. He liked the layout room, where the dummies were prepared. He didn't think much of the linotype machines because they were big and noisy. In the city room were more typewriters than Martin knew existed. He was impressed that his grandfather was the head man in that building.

In June, Eric went to Mexico on business. Stephanie could not accompany him because she was busy with the Pelican Party, so Eric took Linda, Flavia, and Martin with him. The itinerary called for three days at Puerto Vallarta to talk to the naval officers about the new Pacific Fleet, then a weekend in the capital. That was followed by four days at Veracruz, including an interview with the Confederate naval officers there. None of his business was that time-consuming, so he spent a lot of the time with his family. The children constantly practiced their Spanish. Martin picked up an onion in a restaurant and asked the waiter, "¿Señor, como se dice esto legumo?"

"*Una cebolla*, amigo."

FRIED OYSTER SANDWICH

"Ah," said Eric. "Can you see how that is like *Zwiebel?*"

"*Seguramente,*" Martin replied. Then he said to the waiter, "*Asi, como la palabra Alemán.*"

"*No conozco la lingua Alemán.*"

Martin might have continued the discussion, but Flavia gave him a strange look, so he merely replied, "*Gracias.*" The children were as at home in Mexico as they were in New Orleans. On the shore at Veracruz, Eric pointed out to them that across that gulf was Louisiana. The entire journey had been by rail, but from Veracruz they took a ship to New Orleans. In a day and a half, they were home. When they reached home, the children told Renee about the Imperial City, the vast oceans, and the Mexican cuisine. They brought back scented candles. Flavia gave Denise a blue one, and Martin presented Lisa with a silver one.

"Where did you get that?" asked Lisa.

"In Veracruz," said Martin. "I wish you had come with us."

"Was the food good?"

"Of course. The Mexicans make marvelous dishes."

"I wish I had gone too," Lisa said sadly.

Martin felt drawn to Lisa in a new way.

Eric also brought something for Henry. He was a guest on Henry's morning interview program, telling the city about the development of the Mexican navy in response to Japanese naval supremacy. All the diplomats who lived in the city were tuned in that day, especially those from Austria-Hungary. Emperor Charles was dying. He had made a remarkable recovery after his near brush with death twenty-six years earlier, but he was sixty-one now and not at all healthy. He had no living children, so the eyes of the world were on the Mexican who had become his successor, now married to the daughter of Victor Emmanuel III of Savoy. He had been invested as archduke not with the Spanish form of his name, but as Roderick Alexander. The smaller nations of Middle Europe looked to the Dual Monarchy as an ally in the face of the Soviet Union, although at that time Stalin was very careful not to offend Japan, with whom he had a temporary peace. Austria-Hungary was not a great military power; she was still allied with Turkey as she had been during the World War, but Turkey was now a republic, which was more like France, her erstwhile enemy. The Red Army had overrun the nations of the Caucasus during the decade of the 1920s, but they were not at all pacified. The Turks had some ambition concerning the area.

At the next meeting of the Pelican Party leadership, Stephanie discussed relations with the United States. "The population of the Union is moving westward," she said. "Hoover Dam has made electric power more available in Southern California. There's a movement toward statehood for the Pacific territories of Alaska and Hawaii."

"Which means more tension with Japan," said Stanley.

"So there is a new dimension toward their relationship with us," said Henry.

"Those areas are more libertarian than New England or the industrial Midwest," said Johnny Labruzzo.

"Is there still a socialistic spirit in the Union?" asked Stephanie.

"I wouldn't say it's very widespread," said Johnny. "During the Great Depression, there were socialist governors in Pennsylvania, Nebraska, and Wisconsin. But that party disbanded. Those areas are still alienated from Wall Street."

"Then there's the issue of collective bargaining," said Stanley.

"That could bring back some of the tensions of the last century," said Henry."

"You mean the war?" asked Johnny.

"Not really," said Henry. "More likely immigration between our countries."

"Likewise, we have some differences over the central bank," said Stanley.

"And what do we have in common? What things are we in agreement with them about?" asked Stephanie.

"I would say foreign relations," answered Warren McGrory who had been listening silently until they came to foreign policy. "They agree with our relationship with each other, with Canada, and with the European powers. They still differ with us about Mexico, but they share our view of the rest of Latin America. Neither of us know what to do about Japan."

"I think I see an opportunity here," Stanley. "If Japan is a concern for both the United States and Mexico, there could be a common interest to bring them together. At least, we could ask."

"So you think the Pelican Party should try to set that up?" asked Stephanie.

"Definitely," said Warren.

For the last fifty years or so, there had been little trouble with Mexican bandits raiding the north. There was no problem in Texas because cooperation between the Confederacy and the Empire was deeply cherished by both powers. But there were several states of the United States that also bordered Mexico. In the 1880s, some bandits had raided across the border into these. San Diego suffered, as did the towns near the border in Arizona and New Mexico, neither of which was yet a state. The Yankees stationed an infantry division near Bisbee, and a cavalry and infantry division at Yuma. Relations between Empress Carlotta, who was regent at that time, and the United States was not exactly hostile, but they were far from friendly, and there was much less cooperation in the western areas. She appointed her trusted friend Richard Ewell to conduct relations with the country against which he had fought for independence. The empress had no love for the bandits. Although she resented to some extent when Yankee or Confederate troops made unauthorized crossings of the border, she acquiesced when the bandits were turned over to her for justice.

Since 1870, the French no longer had any concern with Mexico. The imperial family had ties with the Dual Monarchy, which made it the European liaison power. It also had ties with England through the Prince Consort, who had died in 1861, and with Belgium, whose monarch was a first cousin to Carlotta. Within the next quarter century, Queen Victoria's many children all married various European royals, which broadened the interests of Mexico in the Old World.

Ewell's mission was completely successful. The US president, Grover Cleveland, who was somewhat partial to the Confederate States, received him in Washington and took his advice in framing a new treaty with the empire. His next stop was at Richmond, where President Simon B. Buckner converted it to a tripartite treaty. The Confederate Congress called for an expeditionary force to be stationed in Texas. There were thousands of volunteers. In less than a year, over eight hundred of the bandits had been killed, and the leaders were in chains in the dungeons of Chapúltepec. The Confederate and Mexican governments took advantage of the occasion to begin a railroad from San Antonio to Oaxaca with a spur line running west to Puerto Vallarta. A second line ran from Veracruz to the capital. Mexico was becoming industrialized.

The bandits tried to assert themselves once more during the World War. The Emperor Carlos was soon in contact with both the Union and Confederate governments. With the help of the railroads, reaction was swift and certain. Stephanie's brother, Danny, saw action in that conflict. That was the last gasp for the bandits. By 1948 the imperial government was so popular that the people themselves acted against the bandits. The Confederates disbanded all the forces that had been involved with them. The Yankees kept only the cavalry division at Yuma.

Fried Oyster Sandwich

Soon it was time to head for Milneburg with the family. Martin and his family, including Patachou, arrived on Friday evening. He had no idea what lay ahead, but he loved the water and dreamed of adventures. He only had to wait until Saturday afternoon for Stanley and Elizabeth to arrive with Lisa. It didn't take long for the four children to don their swim suits. While Henry and Stanley listened to the Pelicans' game on the radio, all four children and Patachou took to the lake.

Denise and Lisa asked Martin if they could try the simulated rescues that the older generation had enjoyed so much. He didn't know how to answer them. He didn't want to refuse, but at age nine, he had little idea how to proceed with it. Flavia intervened. "Mom and Dad were my age when they did that. Dad explained to me once that when Mom was pulling him to the camp, that was the most peaceful feeling he ever had. You kids would have to act to accomplish that," she advised.

"Did they have a dog?" asked Lisa.

"No," Martin answered, "but we do. A dog who wants to swim and play with us."

"Forget the rescues," Flavia encouraged them. "Let's go out to where it's above our heads and swim around."

Martin was a little better at this than the girls. Lisa decided that water above her head was deeper than she wanted to go. "Let's stay closer to the camp," she suggested.

"Okay," said Martin. "Can you get there yourself?"

"Please stay close," she answered. Martin came over to her and helped her. He liked spending time with Lisa, although it was nothing new. Watching out for Denise and her had been his duty for years, especially during the hurricane. But the way she counted on him was very satisfying.

Chapter Eleven

In 1952, June 1 was Whitsunday, the Feast of Pentecost, on which Martin George Kaufmann would be confirmed as a member of the Lutheran Church. Along with seventeen other thirteen-year-olds, he went up the steps on the outside leading to the main entrance to the church, preceded by the pastor wearing a red stole over his surplice. The organist finished the prelude and began the introductory verse of "Come, Holy Ghost, God and Lord." Seven boys and eleven girls kept careful cadence as they marched in rented white robes into the main aisle. They had finished two years of intensive catechesis, meeting three times a week to study the *Short Explanation of Luther's Small Catechism* by Rev. Heinrich C. Schwann, the pastor from Cleveland who'd set up the first Christmas tree in the New World. The congregation remained standing throughout the hymn as the Catechumens reached their reserved seats. They remained standing through the preparatory service, the Introit, Kyrie, Gloria in Excelsis, and Collect. Then they sat down as the pastor read the lessons for the day, rose as he announced the Gospel, and remained on their feet as he read it and the congregation confessed the Nicene Creed. Never had Martin listened so attentively to those words: "Who for us men, and for our salvation, came down from heaven, and was incarnate by the Holy Ghost of the Virgin Mary, and was made man."

That explained why Martin was there. He was a Christian and believed in the Trinity, the Incarnation, and the Atonement. He was baptized in the name of the Triune God. That was objectively true and would never change. He could confess his sins to the pastor and receive absolution, which he had learned from his catechism was "as valid and certain in heaven also as if Christ, our dear Lord, so dealt with us himself." Soon he would receive the Holy Eucharist and partake of the sacrifice by which God "made him who knew no sin to be sin for us, that we might become the righteousness of God in him." The Body and Blood of Jesus would truly, objectively, be in the pastor's hand, then in his mouth. There would be vows to be said today, and he would say them gladly. Two years ago, he had been much less attentive when Flavia was confirmed. The sermon was rather long, about twenty minutes. The ushers gathered the congregation's offerings.

There was a proper prayer of the Church for this Sunday, which took about seven minutes. Then the pastor called the eighteen names, and Martin and his fellow students entered the chancel. The vows they spoke in unison, and then the pastor approached them one by one, spoke their names as the elder rang the bell one time for each name, and spoke the confirmation verse he had chosen for each of them. Then he handed each teenager a certificate. He gave the class a special benediction, after which they returned to their seats as the pastor began the preface. The class would be the first table at communion that day.

After a lot of picture-taking, the family was finally able to return home. But that was just the beginning, because today was Martin's confirmation party. All of his relatives were there, even Henry's Uncle Sam from Tulsa, as well as Renee's cousins from New Iberia. There was a huge dinner, a well-decorated cake, many gifts (including more than sixty dollars in cash), a hymnal, a prayer book, a book about airplanes from Aunt Linda and Uncle Gordon, an astronomy book filled with star maps, and tickets to the movies. Later that day, they went to the nursing home where Essie now lived; her arthritis had gotten the better of her, and so she had retired. The home was a very good one, and Eric and Stephanie paid for it. Essie had stayed away from Eric's confirmation and attended only the party for Henry's, but she blessed the day she was able to see the little ones in the family with whom she had worked, now that its fourth generation was advancing.

As evening came, Martin was the only one who wasn't tired. He felt very spiritual that day. All the guests had departed. His mother wanted Henry to massage her feet, which had served everybody that day. This time, however, she summoned Martin to pay attention in order to learn how to do it. "Martin, your Aunt Linda likes this too, but you can't really ask your father to massage her as well as me. You need to be able to do this."

"Hasn't Aunt Linda gone home?" he asked.

"Yes. But learn it anyway."

Martin perceived some sort of future commitment. He watched the entire ritual and noted how Renee said, *"Merci, mon ami."* He knew what the French words meant, but his father saw his question and explained what that meant in the context of the massage.

He began to see that being a man could be rather complicated. "Would Aunt Linda say something like that to me?"

"No," said his mother, "but I bet Lisa would."

Not only did Martin perceive that every family had layers of agenda in its relations, but hearing Lisa's name in this context caught him off guard. Was his fondness for the younger girl so obvious that his mother knew about it?

The future of the Pelican Party was about to be tested in ways that could not have been predicted. This was a presidential election year, and the party was divided. Stephanie and Eric wanted to support the Conservative Party, whose candidate was W. Kerr Scott of North Carolina, the birthplace of that party. Scott had been elected to the Senate in 1946 as a Conservative. Johnny Labruzzo and Stanley wanted to support incumbent President Albert B. "Happy" Chandler, the Democratic Party candidate. There was a third candidate from the Progressive Party which had lost a lot of ground in the past decade but was still organized in every state. It was the favorite of the oil companies, although the farmers had become disenchanted with it. Henry respected it because of its one great accomplishment, a common currency with the United States. The blue-collar workers, the Pelicans' largest constituency, preferred Chandler. Although they were a local state party, they had influence throughout the Confederacy.

Stephanie wanted to rename the party in the image of the Conservative Party in other states. As they met around the table in the newsroom, there was a long agenda.

"So, Henry, how are the interviews with the candidates going?" she asked.

"They will all be on the air within the next four weeks."

"What is our platform concerning the brown-water fleet?"

"We definitely don't need it any longer," replied Stanley.

"We know ways we can put it to better uses," said Johnny.

Warren nodded in agreement. "We can boost the national treasury by selling the dry docks and administrative buildings."

"The little shallow-draft gunboats can easily be converted into recreational boats," said Stanley.

"Could we use some of it to build a national air force?" asked Stephanie.

She was interrupted by the teletype. Henry walked over to it and then returned grimly to the table. "I'm afraid Mexico is soon to lose its emperor," he said. "His right arm and leg are paralyzed. He has difficulty swallowing."

"We can talk about this after we settle the fleet matter," the chairman continued. "Get back to my question about a national air force."

Warren said, "Well, our country has never had to have a central military. We're more like the feudal system. Every state has its own."

"We have a central navy."

"Yes, because the sea isn't in any state. They are all responsible for it."

"Look at Texas," said Johnny. "It has an air force. Moreover, it wants to buy a couple of the old brown-water fleet buildings."

"There was tension there," said Stephanie. "The men were navy personnel, but some of them became Texas militia instead by transferring to the air force."

Henry was following the discussion, but he had something to say. "We have never considered a central military important. There would be too much chance of 1861 happening among us."

"As far as our party platform goes, though, we are for decommissioning that fleet altogether," said Stanley.

Stephanie took a vote and found the party leaders were unanimous on that point. She went to the next item. "On the presidential election, I believe we should support Scott."

"The factory workers will oppose that. I am certain," said Johnny.

"It would attract the farmers," countered Henry.

"I still think we should support Chandler," said Stanley.

Sides were being taken even as the party leadership looked for a direction. Warren thought the Democrats had more to offer the maritime interests. Mrs. Dumaine, who was usually very quiet, saw Scott as the candidate who best represented the old, aristocratic families. She and Stephanie were at odds with Johnny, Stanley, and Warren. Everybody looked at Henry, who wanted to abstain. As much

Fried Oyster Sandwich

as he wanted to keep the factory workers, he didn't want to lose the farmers. "I believe we need to table this," he said. Stephanie was disappointed in her son but thought she could win him over before the leadership met again. Eric was not there that day, but had he come, he would have had a vote, and he would have voted with Stephanie. Because she was the chairman, she could only vote to make or break a tie. If Henry supported Scott, his vote would make the tie, and Stephanie's would break it.

Johnny moved to table the discussion, and it was tabled. They all had questions about Mexico. Francisco Jose was no longer able to exercise his office. Diego Lopez, Duke of Guadalajara, was now the head of government with the emperor's blessing. There were four imperial children, but none of them were in the loop when it came to official decisions. Henry had a deep interest in Mexican affairs, so much so that he invited Crown Prince Maximillian to New Orleans to interview him on the radio. He was the youngest of the imperial children and the only son. He was twenty-seven years old. He was extremely intelligent, very cerebral, and not very excited about finding a mate. He had a tendency to be frugal. Although he took his destiny very seriously, he was not consulted on all official decisions. The prince would have accepted Henry's invitation had not the emperor taken a turn for the worse. Francisco Jose had a third stroke from which he would not recover. Henry engaged the local Mexican embassy instead. The ambassador was glad to grant an interview.

Henry sat next to the ambassador in the broadcasting studio as the "on air" sign lighted above them. After introducing his guest to the audience, Henry began the interview. "How is the imperial family doing now?"

"The empress is the only one who has been active in public life. The oldest daughter, Maria Cecilia, took religious vows years ago; she is now the abbess of a large convent in Veracruz. The second daughter, Julia, is close to her brother and is quiet and studious. I believe she will be more active in political life. Do you really want to know about Veronica?"

"She's here in the Confederate States, isn't she?"

"Everyone must know that. She lives a Bohemian lifestyle. A few years ago, she moved to Atlanta."

"Isn't she there on some kind of official business?" Henry said.

"That wasn't her plan. She wanted to lose herself in Atlanta, but the press was everywhere. She applied to become a citizen of the state of Georgia. That turned out to be a diplomatic time bomb."

"How was that resolved?"

"President Chandler stepped in and recognized her as an official representative of the Empire of Mexico. He helped the Mexicans open an embassy in Atlanta. Princess Veronica became the ambassadress."

"What did the emperor think of that?"

"He was glad of it and hoped she would take her duties seriously. Time will tell if he was right."

"Now remember, originally I had asked Crown Prince Maximillian to be on the show today. Is he ready to be the emperor?"

"He has good help. Don Diego Lopez is very capable, and the prince knows that. He's very close to his sister Julia; I believe he will eventually appoint her the chancellor. He also corresponds frequently with his sister in Veracruz. She may not be politically active, but the prince values her opinions."

Henry asked, "Do you believe the relations between our countries will be closer than ever?"

"You need not worry about that, my friend."

Fried Oyster Sandwich

The electoral college assembled in Richmond for the presidential balloting. The following day, the Pelican Party leadership met at WOPR's newsroom. By now everyone knew that in a close race, W. Kerr Scott, the Conservative Party candidate, had defeated the democrat Albert Chandler. Lyndon Johnson carried only Arkansas.

"A new era in presidential politics is here," began Stephanie. "The Progressive Party is less relevant than ever."

"What does that mean for us?" asked Johnny.

"I believe that the Conservative Party is the Confederacy-wide affiliate of the Pelican Party," Eric said.

Stanley replied, "If that happens, I will have to leave the party."

"That would estrange the blue-collar workers from the party," said Johnny.

"That's too bad," said Stephanie. "I was going to ask this group to think about renaming our party after the Conservatives."

"Why?" asked Henry.

"Because Pelican sounds like a local interest party. We couldn't be active outside Louisiana."

"Can we put this coalition of constituencies together outside this state?" asked Warren.

"We can't always be a parochial faction," she replied.

"But we can't let other states decide our policies," said Henry.

"Our name denotes a marine bird," said Warren, "preserving the party's image as representing the maritime interests."

"The time is ripe to woo the farmers away from the Progressive Party," said Henry."

Stephanie was aware of the tension her proposal had created. Henry and Stanley were good friends, and she didn't want politics to come between them. If Johnny and Stanley left the party, it would be much weaker. If they stayed, the blue-collar workers would remain, but four years later there would be a more severe test. "Maybe I should resign as chairman," she suggested.

"To whom would you give your resignation?" asked Eric.

"To Henry," she replied. "He seems to want to be the leader, to choose our direction."

"No. You keep the chair, Mother. In a year or two, you might not want to change the name. Everything is changing."

The meeting came to a quiet close, but nobody was happy. "We won't bring this tension home, will we?" asked Henry.

"Nor to Milneburg," said Stephanie. "And Stanley will still come to our family gatherings." Martin and Lisa would be glad of that.

In 1954, the Kaufmann children had become teenagers. Martin, now fifteen, read his grandfather's newspaper and constantly listened to his father's radio station. He and his sister, Flavia, took turns reading the current events magazines. They looked back on the history of the Confederate States since the Treaty of Spotsylvania was signed eighty-nine years earlier, ending the "late unpleasantness."

Everyone knew there had been something of fratricide about the war, and everyone wanted to get over it. As a result, the relationship between the two republics had been completely friendly. The United States of America had benefited from its relationship with its sister commonwealth to the south. Nobody was surprised when the Indian Territory joined the Confederate States. The Cherokee chief, Stan

Watie, had been a general for the Confederacy both in the War of Independence and in the Mexican War. Four battleships had been planned for the Confederate navy, one of them named the *Oklahoma*. None of them had been completed by 1954, but the naval planners had already scheduled her for the Caribbean Fleet. The United States had benefited politically. By making a workable model of a bimetallic standard, the Confederate States had influenced Yankee monetary policy. By remaining out of the World War, they had encouraged the United States to remain non-belligerent as well. By refining large amounts of petroleum, the Confederate States provided fuel for the automobiles that Detroit and Cleveland were so prodigiously producing. Most important, the Midwest and the Far West admired the Confederacy so that the negative influence of New England was minimized. The Jacobinism which had fueled the Union cause during the "late unpleasantness" was now very unpopular. There was still popular election of presidents, and slavery had been abolished everywhere. But the attempt to pass an income tax amendment had failed, and universal suffrage was sent back to the drawing board. Even though the United States had adventured in the Philippines and the Caribbean, its relationship with the commonwealths in both hemispheres that retained the Old Regime was better than ever before. The benefits worked the other way in some cases. The Union helped the Confederacy develop industrially, and they built many railroads in the nation.

The Kaufmann children loved each other dearly. Denise and Lisa were going into the eighth grade and were a year from graduating from grammar school. Martin loved history, music, and geometry. He and his sisters were healthy, intelligent, and socially skillful. He noticed that Flavia had started to talk more about boys. Her favorite subjects were science and literature, and she was editor of the school newspaper. Martin played the clarinet in the marching band. He could talk to Flavia about his fondness for Lisa, and she confided in him her interest in Harold Meyer, from her confirmation class three years ago.

Grandpa Eric was sixty-five now. He and Grandma Stephanie owned the house on Second Street. Henry and Renee lived in Edgewood, and Gordon and Linda lived near the river. At sixty-three, Stephanie still ran the Pelican Party very capably. Eric was considering retirement, for which he was well-prepared. Gordon and Linda were having difficulty with their amateur flight hobby. Air traffic had increased considerably since the late forties. Joy Airport had closed, making it more difficult to rent aircraft. Martin was a bit disappointed that he couldn't fly with them any longer. They had no children but loved hosting one or more of Henry and Renee's.

Essie's health was failing badly. She had not eaten well at the nursing home, so she was malnourished. She had ulcers and began to get frequent headaches. Stephanie visited her every day, but after a week of such attention, Essie passed from this earth. Her funeral was at Holy Redeemer, on Royal Street and Frenchmen. The entire family attended it and stayed for her burial in the churchyard there.

Martin was getting used to living in a constantly changing world. He missed the private plane rentals, and he missed Essie. But most of all, he missed the camp at Milneburg, which the family had sold. The Petersons had also sold theirs, so no one would be going to the lake in the summer. His parents were in tears as they bade farewell to the place they had first met in 1926. That had been their place of retreat; while they were there, they had no worries, not even the year a hurricane hit while they were out there. For Martin, it was a place to be closer with Lisa, and she returned his affection. She was thirteen and lived uptown. The young people wondered whether they could find another meeting place. They did not see each other at church, because Lisa was Episcopalian and Martin was Lutheran. If only they could vacation together!

Then an answer came from an unexpected quarter. Gordon and Linda had invested in a vacation cottage in Mandeville, on the north side of the lake. The grandparents and siblings were invited, as were Dorothy, Stanley, and Elizabeth. They made it plain that the younger generation was invited, even if the parents were not able to come along.

The property was on a small river that flowed across the north part of Mandeville It was copper-colored, flowed with a swift current, and created occasional beaches along its bed. There was one such beach on Gordon and Linda's land; it was only about ten yards long and five yards wide, but it gave excellent access to the river. It was a foot deep, and so one could wade along its length for about half a mile upstream. Downstream, it was not long before the river became deep enough to be navigable. It was well populated with minnows, but little else.

The cottage had four rooms and was shaped like an *E*. The southern bar was a bedroom, and the northern bar was a kitchen. The upright was a large sitting room with a pair of sofa beds, each of which slept two. If the younger generation brought sleeping bags, the six adults would all have beds. The fourteen-year-old Patachou would share the floor with the young folks. There was a small bathroom with no tub, extending from the place where the upright met the lower bar. It was served by a septic tank that emptied from an overflow pipe into a ravine along the north edge of the property. If anyone wanted a bath, one took the hose outside.

The property was basically two parts, the house section on high ground, and the river section about twelve feet lower. In the spring, the river would get rather high, but never as high as the house section; by July it was again confined to its bed. That was the earliest the family ever came, except when they had work to do maintaining it. The cottage was a forty-five minute drive from New Orleans, going over the Watson and Williams Bridge. If two or three of the families were staying there for an extended time, the older generation could always visit for a day.

Lloyd E. Gross

Chapter Twelve

Martin and his family arrived at Gordon and Linda's cottage on a Friday evening in August 1954. He and Flavia laid out their sleeping bags on rugs, and Patachou chose a spot on the rug near Flavia. They were staying for nine days. For Martin, the cottage was a fun place to be, but the prospect of Lisa's arrival the next day brightened it even more. She would also be there the entire nine days.

Every morning, thousands of birds sang a hearty morning greeting. Martin looked forward to hearing the mourning doves, which did not live south of the lake. Every night tens of thousands of crickets sang a background lullaby. There was daily rain from around 2:00 p.m. until around 4:00 p.m. The temperature was in the eighties, and so the children could play outside the entire time. The only potential danger was from venomous snakes, especially the moccasins that inhabited the river. There were a few coral snakes, but there were far more harmless scarlet snakes that looked similar to the coral but with white bellies. The adults always went into the river first to establish that the area was safe. Unless the snakes had moved into the beach area, it was very unlikely that any would appear there.

Martin had no need to rush things. He knew Lisa needed time to play with Denise. While the younger girls played outside, Martin stayed with Flavia. They played chess for a while, and then Martin sat down with a book while Flavia wandered over to the neighboring cottage and discovered four children about her and Martin's age. They were playing on their front porch. Martin put his book down to look outside, and he saw Flavia introducing herself to the next door teenagers. He hurried over to join her as Patachou arrived at Flavia's side.

"My name is Robert," said the oldest. He was tall and fair, of average build, and pleasant looking. He seemed to be older than Flavia.

"My name is Flavia," she answered. "This is my brother, Martin, and my dog, Patachou."

"What breed is Patachou?" Robert asked.

"A Labrador-collie mix," she replied.

Two teenaged girls joined the conversation group. "These are my sisters," said Robert, "April and Betty." Martin knew that April was his age, and Betty was a year younger. Both were wearing shorts and sleeveless tops.

April had light brown hair put up in a ponytail, which stopped above her shoulders. She was wearing flat, strappy tan sandals. "Does the dog bite?" she asked.

"Not our Patachou," said Martin. "I'm Martin, a sophomore at John McDonogh."

"I go there too," said April. "I'm a freshman."

"And I'm Betty, a freshman next year," said the younger sister. She was a blonde with very fair skin and blue eyes. Her hair was short in a pixie cut. She wore tennis shoes and bobby socks. "Are you next door?"

"Yes," said Flavia. "We're the Kaufmanns. We also have a little sister named Denise."

"And we have a little brother," said April. "Here he is now."

"This is Jerry," said Betty.

FRIED OYSTER SANDWICH

The ten-year-old Jerry came outside to join the group. "Have you been down to the beach?" he asked.

"We just came yesterday," said Martin. "We know the way down there."

"Your property has a beach on this side," said Robert. "Ours is on the other side, which belongs to people who live on the next road."

"But they never come down to the river," said April.

"We also have a girl named Lisa with us," said Flavia. "We've known her ever since she was little. She's the same age as Denise."

"You can play on our beach whenever you like," said Martin. "We'll probably go down there every day once our parents tell us it's safe."

"We'd love to go down there with you," said Robert.

"It's getting to be lunchtime," said Betty.

"Yes, we're going to have to go back for lunch ourselves," said Flavia.

"Does your dog swim too?" asked Jerry.

"Of course," Martin answered. "All dogs swim very well."

Martin had always liked Lisa, although now his affection had taken a more romantic turn. He thought back to the time of the hurricane, when Lisa's family had stayed at his house. He was two years older and had looked after Lisa while she was there. He'd cut her food for her. He had buttered a piece of cornbread for her.

"What's that?" she had asked.

"Cornbread," he said. "It's very good."

"My father doesn't like it. He says it's too Southern."

"It won't be long before your father is as Southern as that cornbread," said Martin.

It was fortunate for Martin that Lisa was such a good friend of Denise's. For years, the two had been inseparable, although they lived on opposite sides of town. Lisa did not share Martin's interest in his father's work, even though her father worked with him. She liked dancing and took ballet and tap lessons. Denise went through the motions of dancing lessons, but her heart was at Boutique Bienville with its fascinating world of clothing. Flavia and Martin enjoyed playing bridge.

They went over to the neighbors' house that afternoon to invite Robert and April to their house to play. They met the parents, John and Nancy McKeever. The family lived in the Gentilly area of New Orleans. The children were overjoyed to find bridge players who were around in the daytime, because they could only play with Linda and Gordon in the evenings.

The bridge game was rather makeshift. There was only one deck, and they kept score on used envelopes. It was only rubber bridge, but it might as well have been a tournament where master points were dispensed.

"What does your father do?" asked Martin.

"He owns a tire shop in Lakeview," said April. "We live on Mirabeau, just above Elysian Fields."

"And your mom?" asked Flavia.

"She works in the office at Dad's store," said Robert. "They met when they went to college at Southeastern Louisiana College, at Hammond. She was a cheerleader there."

"You wouldn't believe how our parents met," said Flavia. Rather than beginning the story, she looked at her hand and bid. "One diamond."

Fried Oyster Sandwich

Lisa was uncomfortable with Martin and April as partners at the table. She interrupted the game a couple of times to show off tap steps. Denise led her away.

"Do you know how to play bridge, Denise?" Lisa asked.

"No," she replied.

"Well, I guess I have to get Martin to teach me."

"Good luck," said Denise.

Martin was unaware that Lisa was jealous. He was very fond of Lisa, but he enjoyed playing bridge with April. She was an attractive girl, which he noticed. He did not have a definite place in his mind for two kinds of girlfriends. He would never deceive either of them into thinking they had his exclusive affection.

The next day, the children were playing in the river. Lisa was standing where it was not deep enough to cover her knees, but she gave a little yelp and then called for Martin. "Can you please carry me to the beach?"

"What's wrong?"

"I have a cramp in my toes. I don't want to try to walk." She was thirteen years old; boys her own age were smaller than she was. For the fifteen-year-old Martin, she would not be a challenge. He hurried over to her, picked her up in his arms, and carried her to the beach. He sat on the sand by her feet.

"Which toe is it?" he asked.

"All of them," Lisa answered.

Martin looked at her questioningly. "Which foot?" he asked finally.

Lisa put the right foot in his lap. Martin gently stretched each toe, one at a time. He noticed her nails were painted a pale orange. Lisa groaned. "Hold still," said Martin. "I'm going to massage them." Lisa lay down on her back and closed her eyes while Martin tried to massage her toes. He needed to lubricate his fingers. He looked around for lotion. Finding none, he picked up the sun block and worked it into his fingers.

"What's that for?" Lisa asked. "Are my toes getting sunburned?"

"I don't think so," said Martin. "But you will definitely think this feels better."

Lisa was young, and her nerve endings were at peak sensitivity. Martin moved from her little toe to her big toe and back again, five or six times. There was no more groaning. As he focused on the pads of her toes, he noticed the little ridges, the ones that made Lisa unique. There was something about that he should have remembered. Then it came to him. The footprints that his Grandma Jackie had made, which his mother had framed and hung on the nursery wall. One of those was Lisa's. He considered that if he had those prints now, he might find a match. He put more sun block on his fingers and went back to Lisa's toes. This time she giggled.

"I'm so glad you're here to take care of me," she said.

Was she feeling better? Apparently. He said, "You can probably dance just fine."

Lisa was wiggling her toes without any assistance now. "It will be because of the great massage you gave me. Can you imagine how hard it would be to dance on point with cramped toes?" Martin tried to put her foot down to get up, but she kept it in his hand as best she could. "How do you like my nails?"

Flavia and Denise had gathered around and were looking at Lisa. Martin answered Lisa, "They're girly. That's a good thing, Lisa. You are a girl. It's good for girls to be girly." Even as he spoke those words, he heard himself and considered what he was saying. Then Flavia agreed with that judgment.

Lisa turned to look at Flavia, "I had a cramp in my toes, and Martin took care of me. Nothing makes me feel better than having Martin take care of me."

Now Martin wondered whether or not it was all a game. So what if it was? Lisa had come to him for help. He still did not associate the episode with his playing bridge with April. This was more than a game—it was flirtation, and it was romantic. So far, whatever he did with April was not romantic. But whither would all of this lead?

Later that afternoon, when Martin considered what had happened at the river, he remembered his mother's comment after his confirmation party, when his parents had explained the massaging to him. He didn't expect Lisa to speak French, even though she had learned some of it. He went over to his Aunt Linda and told her what had happened.

"If she were really hurt, I don't think she would have asked you about her nails," Linda advised him. "Everyone knows how much Lisa likes you."

"Do girls always play games like this?"

"Yes," she answered, "but we're not trying to hurt you. Even after we're married, we keep doing things like that. A girl can never stop flirting with her man."

Flavia and Martin liked their new friends, especially because they played bridge. In fact, there was a rather faint spark between Robert and Flavia. The second day they played, the boys were partners against the girls, and third day the Kaufmanns took on the McKeevers. Lisa did not begrudge Martin his card game any longer, but she wanted to learn how to play, so she asked him. He gave her a quick overview of the nature of the game. Then they got together with Flavia, and the two introduced Lisa to the wonderful world of bidding. Denise was not very interested in it, but they knew they would need a fourth once they went home, so they persuaded her to learn the fundamentals.

As for Martin, he was used to being among girls, as he had been all his life. He liked Lisa. He did not resent her little trick, but he thought she was rather foolish for doing it. On the other hand, he was also open to doing things with April. So far, he knew her only as a rather good bridge player. She did not flirt with him, as Lisa always did. She was a year older than Lisa, was slightly taller, and had freckles. They both had dark hair, but April's was considerably longer. Although very reserved, once she got to know people, she became more witty. She would be a freshman at John McDonogh in September, one year behind Martin. Lisa was a year away from high school, but she lived in the district of Alcee Fortier High School. Martin did not try to conceal from either Lisa or April that he enjoyed the company of the other. He did not see any reason to do so.

That was not the case with Lisa. Though it was true that Martin had never called her his girlfriend, she was glad he wasn't playing in the river with April. As for April, the third member of the triangle, she had no idea that Martin might have any interest in her beyond playing bridge.

Martin had frequently talked with his father about natural things. Like his father, he believed that people did not know the natural world. That was more friendly than the post-lapsarian subnatural world. The natural world was moved by mutual love. In the subnatural world, people plotted and schemed to get the advantage over each other. Nature was not to blame for this; man had made it unfriendly. Martin had grown up with a pet. He knew that there was absolutely nothing evil about Patachou. He still had some time to pet her while God gave her life. She was starting to have difficulty walking, but she always greeted him with a lick. She was a precious gift of God. Patachou represented nature as the general phenomenon mankind encounters. He had learned in church that nature was fallen, there were many imperfections within it, and his own relationship to it was flawed. The fall was also within him. He approached life with love of self at the center. But even in this fallen world, there were waterfalls and sunsets, gentle rain and blanketing fog, good food and warm evenings. And there was love.

Love had always permeated Martin's life. There was the simple love of a boy for a pet, which was amply returned. There was the greater love he had for his parents, grandparents, and sisters, especially Flavia. There was erotic love, such as Henry and Renee had for each other. And there was God's love, so aptly described in John 3:16. This was the love that forgave his sins, comforted him when he was sick, gave him courage for times of trouble, and held out to him the hope of heaven. Even if he had been conceived in iniquity like David, he had been born again of water and the Spirit, just like heaven and earth. Therefore his will was not bound any longer, as it had been by nature. God loved him and surrounded him with the Holy Sacraments that made him part of God's people on earth, the people through whom God's love for all was mediated. He expected to someday enjoy erotic love in his own right, and to find even more divine love in it. When he meditated on it, sometimes Lisa was his partner. Sometimes it was just the idea of a woman. Could he imagine April as part of his fulfillment? His fancy never extended to any other particular girl. Some movie stars were very attractive, but he didn't know any of them well enough to consider them that way.

For the rest of the week, the four older teens played bridge every day. Robert gave Flavia his telephone number, and she gave him hers. He had every intention of asking her on a date when they were back in New Orleans. She had gone to her junior prom with Harold Meyer but had not seen him very often since; Harold had called once since then, and they'd talked for about twenty minutes, but he had given her no further encouragement. Robert was new and interesting in a different way. He was less cultivated, but then, so was nearly everybody. The Kaufmanns were extremely refined, and among them Flavia was the most advanced at self-refinement—a capable autodidact. Robert smoked. He could not interest Flavia in that activity, so he brought her a Mounds bar, which she accepted immediately; dark chocolate was her favorite. He kept trying to interest her in the cigarette habit, claiming that it was good for the Confederate economy. But every time she tried to smoke, it made her cough. Flavia couldn't stand that.

Denise did not have any romantic interest at this time. For her, the good life was the time spent at Boutique Bienville. Dorothy and Elizabeth let her model the dresses, even though she did not yet have a woman's figure. She modeled shorts, tops, jackets, cardigans, business skirts, and even some formal wear. If women wore it, Denise was interested in it. Dorothy did not carry swimwear, but there was a shop next door that did; Elizabeth introduced Denise to the owners there. She and Lisa bought the swimsuits they wore in Mandeville there. Both Lisa and Denise were scheduled for confirmation the following spring—Lisa as an Episcopalian, Denise as a Lutheran. The rites were nearly identical.

Eric and Stephanie no longer needed the house on Second Street. They had no pets, and their relatives were busy elsewhere. They lived there with Susie, but she was over fifty now and was working twice a week for another family. One day she informed the Kaufmanns that the other family wanted her full time. Henry and Renee came over with Gordon and Linda to have a farewell party for Susie. Renee cooked more fried fish than Stephanie had ever seen in her life, and everyone was very full. There were shrimp cocktails, hearts of palm salad, and small whole potatoes with garlic and parsley. A fine Chablis from the French Quarter went with the main course, and coffee laced with cognac accompanied the dessert, a mincemeat pie. The younger generation was absent; Lisa and her parents were going to Mobile for the weekend, and the Kaufmann children were at home eating Flavia's jambalaya.

Gordon and Linda were going to move into the house on Second Street. Linda planned to go back to work at WOPR while Gordon expanded his business. He had bought a camera shop of his own, recently adding an employee. The commute would be across town but right on the streetcar line, involving only a transfer at Canal Street. He would still go to the church on Burgundy Street. The car came in handy there, as well as for visiting the cottage in Mandeville. Linda could commute by streetcar as well, transferring at Canal Street to go out to the Jung.

Fried Oyster Sandwich

Eric had retired from the newspaper because he had contracted adult diabetes. With less energy, he was less involved with public life. Stephanie had become the matriarch of the family, as well as being an energetic traveler. She went weekly to Baton Rouge to talk to politicians, appearing on radio and television and speaking at fundraisers. In October, her brother Danny retired from the airline. He came for a long visit, staying with Gordon and Linda, his goddaughter, in the house on Second Street. Then Danny started going with Eric to the cottage for weekends. One weekend Renee brought the children to visit her husband's uncle. They passed the time talking about airplanes, and Flavia and Martin spoke Spanish with him.

The political disagreements, which began in 1952, were not improving at all. Stanley was dissatisfied with the direction Stephanie and Henry were going with the Pelican Party. Stephanie wanted to merge with the Confederacy-wide Conservative Party, which had elected W. Kerr Scott as president. Martin and Lisa did not want to be caught up in the conflict, but their fathers were obviously on opposite sides. When the weekend came and Martin had a chance to talk to Lisa, he brought up the matter.

"It looks as though your dad is joining the Regular Democrats."

"Mr. Labruzzo as well,"

"Because of the factory workers?"

"Of course," Lisa answered. "They were with the Pelicans for the last election, but now the Pelicans are letting them down."

"How are they doing that?"

"My dad says they are. I don't know the details."

Martin put a record on the phonograph for ambiance. He did not want Lisa to focus on the music. "Do you think our fathers will still be friends?" he asked.

"They keep working together at WOPR, don't they?"

"That's what they do for a living. If they want to make a go of it, they have to work together."

"My dad's problem is more with your grandparents," said Lisa. "I think your dad is more neutral."

"Grandma Stephanie has done wonders with the Pelican Party. Now that your dad is a Regular Democrat, I hope we can keep visiting."

"They wouldn't forbid you, would they?"

Martin said, "Of course not. But there won't be as many opportunities."

"Come summer, I'm sure we'll be able to play in the river again."

"The McKeevers will probably be there."

"So you can enjoy both April and me."

Martin started to tell Lisa that it wasn't like that—but was it? The prospect of having both girls with him, even though it came from Lisa, was not an unpleasant one. But would it be for the girls? "I generally enjoy April when I have cards in my hands."

"She's certainly better than I am at bridge," Lisa admitted. "But do you want to kiss her?"

This idea was new to Martin, but it was not unpleasant. Lisa had brought the subject up, and she must have had a reason. "Why? I've never kissed you."

"I know," Lisa said. "When are you finally going to?"

Martin walked over to Lisa and turned her head to him, then gently touched his lips to hers. "I've never done that with April."

Every Friday evening, Martin called Lisa on the telephone. At the beginning of October, he called her to talk about his homecoming dance. "I asked April to go with me."

"Why aren't you taking me?" Lisa asked.

"You're still in the eighth grade. And our homecoming game is against the Tarpons."

"Is school loyalty that important?" Lisa started to sob.

"This doesn't mean April is taking your place."

"It does for the dance," she countered.

"I'm not trying to lead April anywhere. It is a date at the school she and I both attend."

"Well, I hope we beat the Trojans." Lisa sounded petulant.

"Really, Lisa, I need to do this for my own peace of mind."

"Does Denise know you're doing this?"

"I'm not sneaking around, Lisa. I want to keep seeing you, but I have to do this now. That's why I'm telling you directly."

Lisa was too upset to answer him, and she hung up. Martin listened to the silence for while.

Martin kept busy with the marching band, worked hard at his studies, read sports periodicals, and whenever possible kept company with Flavia. He belonged to his church's youth group and soon became an officer in it. On Sunday afternoons, he and Flavia could play bridge with Gordon and Linda. They tried to start a bridge club at their high school but were not successful. They did attract Robert, however, who started dating Flavia.

One of Martin's fellow clarinet players in the band was Jewish. One day when they were improvising after school, his colleague introduced him to klesmer. It was music that thrived among Ashkenazic Jews, including his colleague's family, which was from Russia. They had escaped from the Soviet Union. That in itself was a dreadfully difficult undertaking, but the story was not to end in America; they intended to further migrate to Israel.

A new international fact had emerged. Since before the World War forty years ago, Britain had been committed to establishing a Jewish nation in the area of ancient Israel. This was not popular among the residents of the area, who had been part of the British Commonwealth since the World War; before that, they were part of the Ottoman Empire. Jews were a small minority in the land. To populate it, an enterprise would have to be undertaken to attract Jews from Europe and the Americas. Britain was rather clumsy at this. But in the early 1940s, two Zionist organizations made a major effort at colonization. One of these was more active in Germany and the Dual Monarchy, and the other was in the United States. They had trouble attracting any but the fanatics, although someone discovered that by putting pressure on the Soviet Union, refugees from communism would make great colonists. The regime, led by Josef Stalin and then Nikita Krushchev, was opposed to allowing them to exit, but the group in the United States knew how difficult the Soviet economy was, so it sought to buy freedom for the refugees. As colonists, these people would need leaders from more established Jewish communities. The Zionist groups opened special schools to educate European and American Jews in the concerns of the refugees, urging them to opt for citizenship in Israel.

By the summer of 1946, colonization there had begun in earnest. Britain had set aside a major port area on the Mediterranean for the

FRIED OYSTER SANDWICH

colonists. The settlers called it Tel Aviv, after the settlement on the River Chebar where the prophet Ezekiel saw his vision.

There were a number of Jewish communities in the Confederate States, and the largest was in New Orleans. There was a lot of discussion among them about the new option. There was also a problem for the state department. The new emperor of Mexico stood solidly with his brother, the emperor of the Dual Monarchy, in trying to make emigration a genuine choice for resident Jews in their realms. The same climate held throughout Western Europe in general, though Jewish populations were small in Scandinavia. Most of the Jews in Europe had lived there for centuries; they were represented in all social classes, including the aristocracy. Although most of the settlers came from the working class, their leaders came from the middle class, which included a few Confederates. Among the world's republics, the Confederacy probably had the least anti-Semitism because it had never been through the nightmare of Jacobinism. Similarly, although Poland had been strongly attracted to Bonaparte, it was a more respectable republic, and since its re-emergence after the World War, it kept its distance from France and the Soviet Union. Jews were not uncomfortable in Poland; the rights Bonaparte had given them were still part of the constitution.

This made a lot of air copy for WOPR. Martin was intrigued when his father brought in spokesmen to debate the issues. He listened carefully so he could discuss the matter with his fellow clarinetist. The most interesting facet of this was the plight of the refugees from the Soviet Union. Flavia was interested as well. She wrote a commentary about it for the school newspaper, which her father aired on his station.

By 1956, the Pelican Party had been stripped of half of its constituency. Stephanie had left it the previous year to join the Conservatives. Mrs. Dumaine was no longer active. The leadership had fallen to Henry, and Stanley and Joe had returned to its ranks. It was a presidential year. When Warren arrived, the meeting began. "It seems we have three choices," Henry began. "There is President Scott; George C. Wallace of

Alabama, who is the Progressive candidate; and James O. Eastland of Mississippi, the Democratic candidate."

"The Progressives are now a minority third party," said Warren. "Their candidate is a machine politician."

"He is popular among the blue-collar workers," said Joe.

"That's not enough," said Henry. "This is really a two-horse race."

"And Louisiana may be the deciding state," said Stanley.

"I don't see a first ballot victory," said Warren.

"Scott has the incumbent's advantages," said Henry. "But Georgia, Florida, and the Trans-Mississippi states are solidly for Eastland."

"Are any states divided?" asked Warren.

"We'll find out when the electors meet. My guess is South Carolina won't be all together."

"So where is Scott strongest?" asked Stanley.

"In the tobacco states," Henry replied.

"What about the vice presidency?" asked Joe.

"Your guess is as good as mine," said Henry.

The teletype interrupted them, and Stanley walked over to it. "It seems Princess Veronica is engaged."

There was grief in the Hohenzollern family. Emperor Frederick, who had succeeded Wilhelm II in 1930, died suddenly from a coronary in May of 1956. He was succeeded by his nephew, George I. The new emperor was single, which set in motion a general pilgrimage to Berlin by any royals who had daughters. George was a Lutheran *large dictu*, which meant the kind of general, magisterial Protestant that developed among the Prussian royals in the nineteenth century. This put the idea in Emperor Maximillian's mind that he could safely marry off his sister, Veronica. She was still living in Atlanta, still pursuing a Bohemian lifestyle, and still causing occasional scandals. Veronica was somewhat attracted to becoming a royal. Changing religions was as easy to her as to Henry IV, the first Bourbon. George was attracted to Veronica, and her uncle was already the Austro-Hungarian Emperor. One of the great ironies of history was that the Mexican Hapsburgs rescued two of the European dynasties. All of this was thanks to Richard Ewell and the Confederate Expeditionary Force.

"It appears that it is worth giving up one's chosen identity to become a royal," said Joe.

"All this because we won the War of Southern Independence," said Henry.

"Connect the dots for me," said Joe.

"If we had lost, Juarez would have defeated the empire, Maximillian I would have been executed, and none of the imperial family would ever have been born," said Henry.

"How great is the Providence of God!" replied Warren.

In the course of time, the electors did meet. As predicted, there was no first ballot majority. Mississippi and South Carolina had both been divided. Scott took only the tobacco states, but with Alabama voting for her favorite son, Louisiana joined with the less populous Trans-Mississippi states, and the best they could do was a plurality. Before the second ballot, Tennessee made a deal. It switched from Scott to Eastland when the latter supported Buford Ellington, Tennessee's favorite son, as the vice president. James Oliver Eastland was elected.

Chapter Thirteen

MARTIN WAS A SENIOR AT seventeen. He had matured to the point now that he knew how both Lisa and April fit into his life. April was a year younger and attended Martin's high school. She played bridge very well and was his friend with that common interest. Lisa was two years younger, and she went to a school on the other side of town. Martin had known her since he was a small boy. She had always flirted with him. Lisa was the focus of Martin's romantic interest. He asked her to his senior prom as early as January so there would be no doubts about it. She would have no problem dressing for the event because her mother was the partner of Dorothy Peterson at Boutique Bienville, the women's clothing store where she practically grew up. Lisa was his girlfriend, but he would still see April for playing bridge, and also because her brother, Robert, was now Flavia's boyfriend. They would invite Robert and April McKeever over to play a kind of bridge called Chicago, scored like duplicate but with individual rather than partnership scores kept. Every hand was a new deal, and partners rotated after every four hands. The game was twelve hands or any multiple thereof. It could even be played with a fifth player, going sixteen hands with each player having a bye for four. Martin no longer had any aversion to kissing girls.

Martin was also studying to be a pilot. He never forgot the experience he had enjoyed of flying with Gordon and Linda. He had the patience and equanimity for the academic life. His favorite subjects were economics and history. He and Flavia were both polyglots to the extent that living in New Orleans expedited it, and their German ancestry augmented it. Throughout high school, he played the clarinet. His mother encouraged him to learn other instruments, and he had minimal success with the piano, but not enough to give concerts. Both parents were glad to pay for his private flying lessons.

Martin graduated with honors that spring. When the time came for vacation at the cottage, he and Lisa had things more or less to themselves. Henry, Renee, and Denise were there, but Flavia, Robert, and April all had summer replacement jobs. Gordon and Linda would come the following week, but they would stay with them when Martin's parents went home. The two young people could each practically tell what the other was thinking.

As they walked down to the river the first morning, Martin carried the bundle with the beach towels and the drying towels. Lisa carried the sun block lotion, insect repellent, and a box of cookies. She stood as Martin spread the beach towels on the sand close to each other. "I'll need help with the repellent and lotion," she said.

"I think I can handle it okay."

"Of course—you just have a one-piece bathing suit. But I need help getting under the straps, and under my hair."

Martin didn't care whether or not Lisa was flirting. If she was, he found that very pleasant. If not, he was doing something to help her. "Let's start with the repellent," he said.

That particular aid smelled rather strong. Martin wanted to kiss Lisa's neck as he applied it, but the odor discouraged him. The sun block was less pungent, but it had to cover the same places. "You have the most gentle hands," she said. They waded into the river for about twenty yards. Then Martin turned to look Lisa in the eye.

"I'm going to Tulane in the fall," he told her. "College of Arts and Sciences. I will be in town, but I might not have as much time."

"That's next fall," said Lisa. "We have the whole summer." She wanted to kiss his cheek but got a mouth full of repellent and sun block. "Is there a better way to do this?"

"There are lots of boys where you go to school," Martin continued. "Are there any that might turn your head in their direction?"

"The same ones that have been there the last two years. None of them have turned it yet."

"I have no worries about your intentions, Lisa. Those temptations are always around. We will need to be patient."

"For that matter, there will be plenty of girls at Tulane. But none of them cause me any concern."

The water was only a foot deep. They were past the point in their relationship where they might enjoy splashing one another. Instead, they sat down in the river to enjoy its coolness. After a few minutes, they walked back to the beach. Denise was just getting there. Martin and Lisa loved Denise dearly. She was clearly a third party here, but they welcomed her. They watched Denise open the box of cookies and take three. Martin dried himself off, but Lisa, always the flirt, waited for Martin to help her.

As the sun declined in the west, Martin took Lisa by the hand and led her to the spot he had previously picked out. At the very western edge of the property was a pine tree about twenty feet high, and it was quite full. He gestured for Lisa to sit and sat beside her. "I remember how beautiful it is to watch the sunset here," he said. "I call this my tree. Mom and Dad ignore it, but I love it."

"So we watch it set here?" she asked.

"Try it; you'll like it," Martin answered.

FRIED OYSTER SANDWICH

After a few minutes Lisa asked, "Do you want me to learn your religion, Martin?"

"You mean more than I've taught you over the years?"

"Yes. I look at your parents, and they never miss a Sunday. Mine haven't gone to church since my confirmation."

"Have you talked to them about it?"

"I've asked them, but I don't think they know. They don't seem to have time for it."

"In a way, I'm surprised that they kept their membership. They identify with blue-collar workers, but the Episcopal Church is more of a country club denomination. They probably never joined any clubs or anything there."

"Your father sings in the choir. Your mother cooks for church dinners. And you go to your Walther League—last year, you were the president of it."

"Why don't you come with me when we get back?" he suggested.

"I don't drive. You'd have to come get me."

"I'll be very glad to do that."

Lisa rested her head on Martin's shoulder. After a couple of minutes, he leaned over to kiss her. She took his head in her hands to prolong the kiss. They remained silent as the last rays of the sun disappeared. Then they walked back to the house arm in arm.

Renee was certain by this time that Lisa would become her daughter-in-law, and the idea excited her. In a way, it brought her lifelong friendship with Dorothy Peterson full circle. She shared this thought with Henry, who was glad that Martin was courting Stanley's daughter. The reaction from Stanley and Elizabeth was even more positive. They knew their only child would be well off with Martin, no matter what he did. They were happy that Denise would be Lisa's sister-in-law. Nobody gave much mind at this point as to what church the couple would attend. In time, that would take care of itself.

Eric had become anemic at sixty-seven. He had little energy for daily tasks and delegated the driving to Stephanie. He loved spending time with his grandchildren, and he did volunteer work for the church, helping to count the offerings. He and Stephanie purchased half of a duplex on Esplanade Avenue, not far from Beauregard Circle. They had a second bedroom in which Flavia came to live when she wasn't in school. Sometimes the three of them would spend a Saturday afternoon taking the ferry to Algiers, having lunch there, and then taking the ferry back to the east bank. Flavia followed in Henry's footsteps in regard to his love for fried oyster sandwiches. Soon Robert became a fourth for these occasions, and he occasionally picked up the tab. Robert was fond of horse racing, and he persuaded them to spend some Saturdays at the nearby Fair Grounds during the racing season.

Martin and Lisa were engaged before Martin finished Tulane. Stanley and Elizabeth were glad to have him in the family. About that time, Maurice retired. When he did, he and Jacquelyn sold the house on Claiborne Avenue and moved to a bungalow in Chalmette. The family Thanksgiving feast moved from Eric and Stephanie's to the Gautiers'. There was shrimp remoulade, gumbo, *grillades,* fried speckled trout and soft-shelled crabs, and oysters any way one wanted them.

Martin had another surprise for Lisa. He had managed to rent a plane at New Orleans Airport out in Lake Pontchartrain. It was just a Piper Cub, with a ceiling of about six thousand feet, but he found that a perfect elevation to propose marriage. When she accepted, he made a loop that frightened Lisa. "Cut that out!" she yelled at him.

Fried Oyster Sandwich

"Don't you want to celebrate?" he asked her.

"I would prefer a celebration that keeps my lunch in my stomach."

"I have to admit, that's a compelling argument," Martin replied. He banked to the left and made a full turn. Then he returned to the airport. He drove her to his house, led her up to his room, and took out a diamond ring.

"Now you have to come to my house," Lisa insisted. Martin drove across town while Lisa admired her ring. When they arrived, she led him up to her room, got out a pair of pointe shoes, and waved them at Martin. "Put these on me," she said. 'I have a perfect choreography for this occasion." She sat on the bed while Martin knelt at her feet, removed her flats, secured the lamb's wool toe guards over her toes, fitted the pointe shoes on her, and laced them up. "Now watch this!" she said, and she performed a solo she had learned for her ballet school review.

"You are great at this," Martin proclaimed.

On the longest day of the year, June 21, 1963, the families gathered in the ballroom of the Jung Hotel to celebrate the wedding of Martin Kaufmann and Lisa Kozar. The ceremony had been that afternoon at the Lutheran Church on Burgundy Street. Now the couple greeted their guests as they arrived. The Jung was air-conditioned now.

"I was wondering whether this day would ever come," said Stanley.

"It seems that patience was rewarded," said Renee. "Not that anybody wouldn't have predicted this."

As Stanley moved over to the bar, Maurice and Jacquelyn joined their daughter. "My grandson sure chose a lovely bride," said Jacquelyn.

"He waited long enough," said Maurice.

"He had to finish his commitment to the air militia," said Eric, who was just joining in.

"A true weekend warrior," said Jacquelyn. "Meanwhile, he worked for his grandfather's newspaper."

Denise was the maid of honor. She stood next to Jacquelyn as Maurice went to talk to the bride and groom. "My brother loves to write," she said. "Is everything settled as to where they'll live?"

"Lisa was working on a medal at ballet school," said Jacquelyn. "I think they found a place just uptown from the Garden District."

"You should see her dance," said Renee. "I bet she could be a prima."

"And Martin should be an economist," said Eric. "I know he likes the paper, but I expect he's not finished with school yet. He's probably waiting for a teaching fellowship."

"You're optimistic, Grandpa," said Denise.

"I've found that life is more pleasant when you are. Now, excuse me," he said as he went back to join Stephanie, who was talking to the bridesmaids.

Stanley came back with Elizabeth. "What are you folks talking about?" Elizabeth asked.

"Neither fiscal nor monetary policy," Renee replied, referring to Martin's favorite subjects.

"Or politics," said Stanley, "which is your husband's favorite."

The room grew quiet as Robert McKeever, the best man, called for attention. "Welcome, everybody," he said. "Before we start our program, I propose a toast." He hesitated for a few seconds and then continued, "Martin and Lisa: a couple who were made for each other."

The bridesmaids in their yellow dresses came together in front of the photographer. Martin and Lisa went onto the dance floor for the first dance. Stanley waited patiently for the second dance with his daughter, but he started moving toward the music.

"How exactly did they meet?" asked Elizabeth.

"Ever since they were born," said Renee.

"Since Lisa was born, anyway," said Jacquelyn. "She's two years younger."

Dorothy joined the group. "The dresses are really wonderful," said Renee, acknowledging that they were from Boutique Bienville.

"I believe the shoes were from Mr. Phillips on St. Claude Avenue," said Dorothy.

"I usually got my children's shoes there," said Renee. "Especially Flavia's, because she was a little hard to fit. But I had to get Lisa's ballet shoes at Ford's on St. Charles Avenue."

Jacquelyn excused herself to leave the group. She found Maurice and prepared him to join her when the general dancing began. Eric and Stephanie came over to them. "This all started thirty-seven years ago," said Stephanie, "when Henry met Renee at Milneburg."

"And it took a major turn when Henry hired Stanley at WOPR," Maurice added. The bride and groom finished their dance, and Lisa sought out Stanley for the bride-father dance.

While Martin had a moment to himself, he went to visit with Flavia. She was also a bridesmaid, wearing a long, yellow dress with chartreuse shoes. "It's great to have the whole family here," she said. "We need more weddings in the family."

"I understand yours is coming up soon," said Martin.

"In six weeks," Flavia replied. "Robert is going to be in charge of a new store his father is opening."

"Didn't he just get the mid-city store a year ago?"

"Yes, but now they're going to open one in New Iberia. Grandma Jackie says she's moving back there, and he thought he would like to relocate near her."

"She has such a nice place in Chalmette."

"They've been in New Orleans since 1920, when Grandpa Maurice came to work on that bridge."

"And our cousins all live there."

"I checked it out. I can work at the library there; they need someone to assist with translations."

"Well, we'll have to rent a plane and fly down to see you."

"It's a pretty trip by car."

"True, but it takes half the day getting there."

Martin and Lisa found a place to live just uptown from the Garden District, on Napoleon Avenue, close to St. Charles. They were only a streetcar ride from Stanley and Elizabeth's.

Epilogue

MARTIN AND LISA DID NOT stay very long in New Orleans. In 1964, Martin was offered a teaching fellowship to pursue doctoral studies at Vanderbilt University. He and Lisa moved to Nashville, where Lisa worked as a teaching assistant at a ballet school. He received his PhD in 1968 and remained at Vanderbilt as an associate professor. Martin thrived in the academic environment.

Flavia married Robert McKeever, with whom she moved to New Iberia, the home of her mother's parents, to open a branch of the family tire store. They had two sons: George, after Flavia's great-grandfather, and John, after Robert's father. Flavia worked at the public library, assisting with translations among the many languages she had learned.

Gordon and Linda invited Henry and Renee to invest with them in the house on Second Street, where the two siblings and their spouses continued for the rest of their lives. They transferred to Zion Church on St. Charles Avenue, where Eric had been confirmed. They continued to meet with Stanley and Elizabeth every week at the Café du Monde, and they enjoyed playing canasta. Every summer they spent two weeks at the cottage in Mandeville with Dorothy. Denise became Dorothy's partner at Boutique Bienville.

The older generation remained active in their children's lives. Eventually, Maurice and Jacquelyn moved back to New Iberia, where they could spend more time with their granddaughter. Eric and Stephanie were very comfortable on Esplanade Avenue. They also went to Mandeville every summer, and to the house on Second Street for all the family holidays.

Martin became well-known in academic circles, especially because he could read Latin and Greek. Eventually he was offered a full professorship at Louisiana State University in Baton Rouge. Media people were constantly seeking his opinions on economic matters, questions of Louisiana and Confederate history, and especially the subject of Mexico. While living in Baton Rouge, Martin and Lisa had two children: a boy named Eric, after his great-grandfather, and a girl named Elizabeth.

In 1977, Martin became the standard-bearer for the Conservative Party in the gubernatorial election. On election night, the family gathered with the party leaders for news of the returns. There were even a few members of the old Pelican Party, which had dissolved in 1957. Joe Labruzzo, the labor leader, came up to Martin to thank him for standing by the blue-collar workers. Lawrence Kraemer, who worked with Martin's father and father-in-law at WOPR, was on hand. As for Martin's grandparents, Eric was now eighty-eight and Stephanie was eighty-six, but they still made their way from their house on Esplanade Avenue to see their grandson's election. Maurice had died four years earlier, but Grandma Jackie sent a telegram from New Iberia, where she lived in a room in Robert and Flavia's house.

Early returns were mostly from New Orleans, Baton Rouge, and Shreveport. The election was very close in those places. Martin knew his strength would be with the farmers and the maritime interests in New Orleans. The factory workers were divided among the two candidates. He and Lisa got up from their table and walked over to Stanley and Elizabeth. Although Martin's in-laws had joined the Democratic Party in 1956, they voted for Martin now and encouraged him. "This will be great for Louisiana," said Stanley.

"And for the Confederate States in general," said Lisa.

"Who would have believed this when we were in Nashville?" asked Martin.

Fried Oyster Sandwich

Henry and Renee walked over. They were both Conservatives now. "I'm very optimistic," said Henry.

"We all are," said Elizabeth.

Returns came in from Monroe and Farraday, which favored his opponent. "We're slightly behind now," said Renee. "This is bad for my nerves."

Four different channels had their news broadcasts on, making it difficult to hear what was being said, but the screens showed visuals of the results. Nobody was trying to call this election.

Lake Charles, Alexandria, and Bunkie reported. There had been no change in the race. Martin had carried Houma handily, and he was doing well in Nachitoches. "That was a surprise," said Henry. "You're doing better than predicted in the west."

"Lisa and I spent two days campaigning there," said Martin. "Especially Nachitoches. But I'm really expecting to do well in Lafayette."

By 10:30 p.m., Martin was moving ahead. The downtown wards of New Orleans, where there were still plenty of Germans, supported him. Returns from the western parishes generally helped his opponent, but most of the others were favorable. The west bank of Baton Rouge was solidly for Martin. All the votes were evenly spread along racial and religious lines.

By 11:30 they were hearing from the North Shore. Hammond, Pontchatoula, rural St. Tamany Parish, and Tangipahoa Parish had become Conservative strongholds. For the television pundits, Bogalusa was the tipping point. They began to project that Martin would be the new governor. The waiters started clearing a place to put up a lectern. Midnight passed, and by 12:30 newspeople were interviewing Martin so intensely that he didn't have time to hear the returns. He did not know his opponent had conceded, but Lisa did. She came up to Martin and kissed him on the cheek. "Congratulations, Mr. Governor," she said. It was true.

The whole family gathered around Martin and Lisa. "I wonder what Grandpa George would think of this?" he said into the microphone. "A hundred years ago, he was captain of the Jackson Avenue Ferry. We Kaufmanns have been around for a while. My grandfather, who edited the *Picayune* and fought so fiercely for good maintenance of the levees. My father, who founded WOPR and knew the Mexican imperial family. My grandmother Stephanie, who was the first chairman of the Pelican Party. My aunt and her husband, who taught me to fly. My sainted grandfather Maurice, who helped build the Watson and Williams Bridge. They can all look on this hour and say their work was not in vain."

"And that's just the past," said Renee. "I look at my son, my daughter-in-law, and my grandchildren, and I have hope for the future of Louisiana."

"Should we wake them up and tell them?" asked Lisa.

"Not now," said Martin. He put his lips to Lisa's. "I could never have done this without this fine lady."

"Are you looking to seek further offices?" asked Joe.

"Please, let's exercise this one first," said Martin. "The best thing we can do for our country now is to govern our state well. I will need everybody's help for that, but I have nothing but confidence in this group. For now, let's celebrate what we have achieved. I'm certain that there is a lot more to come."

Appendix A

How the South Achieved Independence

Pap Thomas was dead. The best tactical commander in the Union Army had been killed as he rallied his men, assaulting the Confederate position on Missionary Ridge. Twice his corps had ascended the heights; twice they were repelled. He led them himself as they went one more time against the entrenched position. A rifleman took careful aim at the leader and fired. Thomas's corps became demoralized and returned to their position in Chattanooga. John Breckinridge's tired division had given their all and held, despite dreadful losses. William Hardee's division, on Breckenridge's right, had held off a less forceful attack by William T. Sherman's corps. The siege would continue.

Another attempt to break out was being made against General Stevenson's position on Lookout Mountain. This was led by General Joseph Hooker, sent down from the Army of the Potomac, for the latter expected no attack from Lee, whose ranks were badly reduced at Gettysburg. Although few Confederates opposed him, they held the high ground. For hours, Hooker made a number of half-hearted attempts. By mid-afternoon, Bragg sent Longstreet's men to reinforce the Lookout Mountain area. They arrived at Stevenson's right just as Hooker was trying to flank him on that side. A bitterly discouraged Hooker retreated to the city.

A new army had been organized in Cincinnati: the Army of Ohio, under General John Schofield. This had been conceived by General Ulysses S. Grant as a reserve for the West, after he had split the armies of the Tennessee and Cumberland, the former to attack Atlanta and the latter to hit Knoxville. Schofield's formation would advance to Nashville, from whence it could move either southeastward to follow up Sherman's advance, or southwestward should a Confederate threat appear from Mississippi. In December, rains caused the rising of the rivers in Kentucky and Tennessee. Schofield thought that was a useful occurrence, and so while he proceeded by rail to Nashville with his headquarters and the artillery, he sent the infantry by river to where the Tennessee became less than navigable at Muscle Shoals. He had hoped that he could reassemble the army on the upper Tennessee, which was simple enough, but there was no river transport there. The flotilla returned to Cincinnati to be refitted, and Schofield's division commanders met to consider what they should do. They built pontoon bridges, crossed the river, and moved to Athens on the north bank. As soon as Schofield was aware of the situation, he ordered his infantry back to Nashville to join him. The Army of Ohio was together again by early February, and the situation in Chattanooga became critical.

With the death of George Thomas in November and the failure of Hooker's attack on Lookout Mountain, the army group was slow to react to the very real threat as the Confederates crossed the Tennessee. During the week after Christmas, Polk's division was recalled from Mississippi, had moved around the Confederate left, and was taking a position on Raccoon Mountain. Communications by way of Moccasin Bend had been broken. The railroad from Knoxville had been broken by Forrest's men, even though General Ambrose Burnside held the town. Hardee's division was entrenched on Missionary Ridge; Wheeler's cavalry was the Confederate right wing. Bragg still had Longstreet's division, although Lee beseeched Davis to have him returned to the Virginia theater. Bragg needed that division to hold Lookout Mountain. There was nothing left otherwise but a semitrained brigade of Georgia militia, which was ill-equipped. Breckinridge's division had been badly mauled. Stevenson's detachment was a less than full-strength brigade.

No order came from Richmond, so Bragg kept Longstreet, and the Union army group remained besieged. As January and February passed, the supply situation in Chattanooga deteriorated.

Grant wanted to try another assault, and he had the best reputation in the Union army. He had beaten A. S. Johnston and Beauregard at Shiloh, Van Dorn at Corinth, and Pemberton at Champion's Hill and Vicksburg. He was less popular with the men because he was willing to sacrifice their lives to destroy Confederate formations. There was sufficient ammunition for the infantry, although the artillery was running short because of intermittent dueling with the Confederate artillery in the Missionary Ridge area. Grant knew he had the Confederates outnumbered, but he was unaware of the overall strategic situation. He did not know that Steele still held Memphis, that McPherson held Vicksburg, and that Banks had taken Port Hudson. He knew for a fact that Forrest was moving freely all around Tennessee. Although Schofield's army had been his idea, he had no intelligence of its presence at Nashville. He ordered an assault on the area where he thought he had the best chance of success: Raccoon Mountain and the Confederate left. As soon as Longstreet was aware that no simultaneous attack was coming against him, he moved to reinforce Polk.

The Army of the Cumberland took heavy losses that day. Grant moved units from his left to his right. Wheeler soon noticed that there was nothing to prevent his fording the Tennessee in his front, and his cavalry took a position on the northwest bank. This area was not difficult for the Union to reach, so they sent a division across the river by one of their ubiquitous pontoon bridges. Eventually the superior Union forces drove Wheeler back to the Confederate main line, but Grant reacted to the threat on the left by weakening his center. Bragg would not let Hardee move; he thought it was a trap. A second day of attacks passed, and the tactical situation was the same as before the battle began. Bragg ordered the Georgia militia up, and had Grant attacked a third day, they would have been necessary. But the Union's ammunition supply had become the critical factor.

Grant waited a week for relief from Nashville. Schofield was unaware that Grant was expecting him to move, and he had no orders. He knew Forrest had passed through the Duck River valley in February. He thought he could help by pursuing him. He sent a division to try to pin Forrest against the Tennessee River, while the flotilla moved behind him. Forrest did not cooperate and moved due south instead of west, soon reaching the upper Tennessee at Decatur. The flotilla, unable to navigate Muscle Shoals, could not get there. Schofield could, but Forrest retreated to Huntsville. The week went by, and Grant sent a white flag to Bragg to negotiate. Ninety percent of the enlisted men and 75 percent of the officers were paroled at once. The Confederates would not have been able to feed all those prisoners, but all the weapons fell to the Army of Tennessee. Chattanooga was once again in Confederate hands. Grant himself was among the prisoners, and two Union armies no longer existed. Bragg telegraphed Davis, and immediately the latter ordered Longstreet back to Virginia. Bragg set out with the rest of his army after Schofield, who returned to Nashville because he could not afford to lose the city. By that time, Forrest was at Florence, on the lower Tennessee.

March 15, 1864, would be a red-letter date forever on the Confederate calendar. Not only had Chattanooga been returned to Confederate hands, but over seventy Parrot rifles, twice that many smaller field pieces, about two dozen howitzers, and a trainload of small arms had been captured. These were taken to a makeshift depot in Atlanta, where representatives of all the Confederate armies could come to claim the prizes. Three of the most capable Union generals, Grant, Sherman, and Rosecrans, were prisoners on their way to Richmond.

Washington learned about the defeat within a few hours, largely through espionage. They sent a telegram to Schofield ordering him to attack Bragg. Schofield was still on his way to Nashville, where most of his artillery was. He hurried to Nashville as soon as he received the telegram, but it would be May before he could make any kind of offensive. Without Longstreet, Bragg's army was about the same size as Schofield's, and it held the high ground. As if that weren't enough, when Longstreet arrived in Virginia, Davis sent S. D. Lee with two brigades to reinforce Bragg, so there was equilibrium on both fronts. Schofield physically moved to where he could contact Bragg's army, but he refused to fight a battle. He appealed to Halleck to send Burnside from Knoxville to help him. Halleck replied that Burnside was no longer in the west. He had been recalled to command a corps in Meade's army.

The strategic situation had been severely compromised, but the Union still held some high cards. The blockade continued; the Mississippi and Tennessee Rivers were firmly in the Union's grip. Schofield held Nashville and was unlikely to risk it as he moved after Bragg. On the other hand, the diplomatic situation had been greatly altered. The French, committed to Maximillian and Carlotta, hated Lincoln's aid to Juarez. Although they had no desire to act without the assistance of England, they definitely favored the Confederate cause. Since the death of the Prince Consort in 1861, Queen Victoria had withdrawn herself from the activities of government. She was appalled by some Union activities, particularly those of General Benjamin Butler, but because of the Prince Consort, she was partial to abolition. Even after his death, she chose to honor him by despising the Peculiar Institution. Parliament saw no real advantage in recognizing the Confederates because the blockade prevented any substantial trade with them. However, now that the queen was too depressed to interfere, and the Confederates had shown a military advantage, Parliament was opening discussions with the French again. Russia remained committed to the Union. The middle European powers had few dealings with America. Spain was divided by internal conflict.

In Virginia, George Gordon Meade commanded the Army of the Potomac. He was the victorious hero of Gettysburg. Lincoln held him at arm's length because of his lack of energy in pursuing Lee's battered units, but Lincoln could turn to no one else. He had Burnside's corps recalled from Knoxville, leaving it in the hands of Union-friendly militia. The losses of Gettysburg were slowly being replaced, and the army reorganized. Hancock's and Sedgewick's corps remained as they had been. The Fifth Corps was now under the command of General

Governour Warren, Burnside's Ninth Corps was once again in Virginia, and General Philip Sheridan commanded Meade's cavalry.

On the south bank of the Rapidan sat the Army of Northern Virginia, unmoved since August 1863. Meade had kept it from getting too comfortable by an attack at Mine Run, which Lee was able to repulse, but only just. The weather became impossible for movement, and slowly but surely, Lee's army integrated its replacements. It once again had the three corps that served at Gettysburg, as well as Stuart's cavalry. Its strength was about two-thirds of what Lee had led into Pennsylvania nine months earlier, but it was well fortified in its position. With the situation at Chattanooga resolved, Richmond was sending nearly all of the replacements to Lee. By mid-April, several batteries of smoothbores had been upgraded to Parrots. However, Lee would never take the offensive again. He knew that the river upgraded his position, so he would not leave it unless forced to do so.

To the west was Joseph E. Johnston at Meridian. Completely recovered from his 1862 wound, he now commanded the Department of Alabama, Mississippi, and East Louisiana. He had few troops, and thus he depended on Forrest for any kind of offensive options. It is possible he could have defended Meridian had McPherson made a half-hearted attack against it from Jackson. McPherson had left most of his army at Vicksburg because of the possibility of Confederate action coming from the Trans-Mississippi. The fortunate Johnston remained in place, received new ordnance, and slowly built up his strength. The Union had a major force at Memphis, Frederick Steele's corps and Benjamin Grierson's cavalry. These were also uneasy about leaving the river.

Bragg was north of Chattanooga with his right flank anchored on the town of Manchester, which was occupied by Wheeler's cavalry. His left flank rested on lakes, with S. D. Lee's two brigades next to them. Breckinridge's division was so badly mauled that Bragg decided not to rebuild it. Breckinridge was given a command in defense of Charleston, and Carter Stevenson took over his old command; it served as a reserve. Next to Lee, Polk was fully recovered and much better equipped than he had been at Chattanooga, and he held the left-center while the relatively fresh and rested Hardee held the right-center. Bragg fortified this position. Schofield made contact with it already in March but refused to engage it. He could not turn it, it would be foolish to assault it, and he was popular with his men as long as there was hardly any shooting. He was between Bragg and Nashville, but he doubted that Bragg would attack him. A new brigade had arrived of four Michigan regiments, which reinforced Nashville itself.

Since early in 1862, most of the Trans-Mississippi had been lost to the Confederates. Samuel Curtis had beaten Earl van Dorn at Pea Ridge, placing Missouri into Union hands and soon capturing Little Rock. Apart from Stan Watie's Cherokees, the only solid resistance west of the river was along the Red River, particularly at Shreveport, under the command of General Richard Taylor, son of the ex-president. Lincoln had ordered Nathaniel Banks, his commander in New Orleans, to move against Taylor. Banks waited.

By May, Meade was ready to move against Lee. Stanton wanted to coordinate offensive moves in all theaters of the war. He outfitted a corps under Henry Slocum to make an amphibious attack against Charleston, to coincide with Meade's move. He also ordered Schofield to attack Bragg. Further west, a new Union division under the command of Samuel Sturgis was waiting in Memphis with Grierson's cavalry to undertake an expedition against Forrest. The latter was very hard to pin down. He was a threat to cut the rail line between Nashville and Schofield's army. He would appear anywhere between Decatur and Tupelo, once being sighted as far north as Clarksville, on the Cumberland. Johnston remained at Meridian, where he had collected a reinforced brigade under General Hyland Lyon, Phillip Roddey's brigade of Forrest's men, Colonel Edward Crossland's Kentucky brigade, and two new units under Colonels Tyree Bell and Hinchie Mabry (militia as far as training, but equipped with the prizes from Chattanooga, the Sharps rifles). Johnston's sparse foot artillery was with Lyon. All of the horse artillery in the department was with Forrest. Sturgis was aware that Forrest's supply line led to Johnston, but he could not move directly against Meridian without exposing his flank to Forrest's attacks. The country was heavily wooded. If caught in column, Sturgis's command would be destroyed.

In the trans-Mississippi, Banks made his move in April, engaged Taylor for about a week, fought two battles, and then retreated back to New Orleans. Sturgis waited. Schofield and Bragg faced each other at Manchester, neither willing to attack the other's position. But at the beginning of May, Meade launched a major campaign against Lee on the Rapidan.

The story of the Wilderness has been told many times: How Hancock pushed A. P. Hill's men on the Orange Plank Road, while Warren and Sedgwick stalled in front of Ewell on the turnpike. How, when Hill's men were about to retreat, Longstreet showed up on the Confederate right and attacked immediately. Some sources even speak of Gordon's move against the Union left. It was a very short hook, but it caused the careful Sedgwick to call off his attacks. Meade learned of it and feared an enveloping move, even though all of the Army of Northern Virginia except the cavalry was accounted for and engaged. As Hancock's corps retreated before Longstreet, Meade feared that he would lose his army, and he withdrew to the north bank of the Rapidan.

The last link in the chain of attacks that Stanton and Halleck had carefully planned was the amphibious action at Charleston. Slocum landed his men south of the city, in the swamps. They made little progress, but neither did they go away. By June, they were in contact with Breckinridge's defenses. Sturgis made his move about that time and was defeated by Forrest at Brice's Crossroads. The war for Southern Independence was getting bogged down.

Soon the time came for political conventions, with which the Union was encumbered, and from which the Confederates were free because they had placed their leaders for the duration of the emergency. In 1864, it was a presidential year. That particular election would be a referendum on the war. General Jubal Early besought Lee to give him the Second Corps of his army to serve as a Valley Army, which he would use to threaten Washington. Lee refused because Meade outnumbered him on the Rapidan as it was. Whereas Early's plan was simply the Chancellorsville plan on a grand strategic scale, Lee now thought that Washington was far more vulnerable to the northern voters than it was to his troops. The eager Early had a sound idea, but naturally he deferred to the wise Lee, who by now had become a demigod to the Confederacy.

Two new Confederate divisions were commissioned in late June, one under General William Loring at Selma, Alabama, and the other under General A. P. Stewart at Augusta, Georgia. Both had seen action earlier in the war—Loring with Pemberton at Champion's Hill, and Stewart with Bragg at Perryville, Stone's River, and Chickamauga. Davis sent Stewart to reinforce the defenses of Charleston. Meanwhile, he hesitated about Loring. Added to Bragg's army, he might make them strong enough to attack Schofield. Added to Johnston's force, he might make them strong enough to move against Memphis. There was a direct rail connection to Meridian from Selma, and Davis decided to send Loring west.

July brought the most welcome news of all. On the first anniversary of Pickett's disastrous charge, Napoleon III recognized the Confederate States of America as a sovereign nation. He met with Secretary Judah P. Benjamin in Paris and then arranged for a division to occupy Nassau in the Bahamas, a base that had been leased from Britain. Along with the division, commanded by General Achille Bazaine, he sent warships. The Union navy would have to keep its distance or else risk war with France.

There were immediate repercussions in Europe. Russia sent a letter of support to Seward, Lincoln's secretary of state, and a diplomatic protest to Elyseé. Austria-Hungary, France's enemy in Italy, also sent encouragement to Washington. Prussia, under the watchful eye of Otto von Bismarck, would not act until England did; he had an iron rule that Prussia must always be in the majority among the five powers of Europe. He was more at home with the industrial North than with the agrarian South, but he was planning an invasion of Bohemia that would put him on the other side from the Austrians. England held all the cards.

In spite of their abolitionist sentiments, which could be furthered by diplomatic rather than military means, they were disappointed at the military ineptitude of the Union. Popular sentiment in England favored the Confederates. As for the queen, she still mourned her Albert, but she was a blood relative of Carlotta. She would not act against France in the Mexican matter, with which Southern independence had now become entangled. Although the popular sentiment among the Prussians was pro-Union, the ruling class was committed to Maximillian and Carlotta. Europe abounded with secret messages between embassies. Secretary Benjamin traveled to London. The bankers and industrialists, who favored the Union, were pitted against the common people and the queen. Even the industrialists understood the importance of cotton. Benjamin prevailed. On July 25, Parliament recognized the Confederate States of America. Bismarck then joined the Russians and Austrians, secure in the conviction that France and England would take care of business because they were the primary maritime powers. He sent them secret messages guaranteeing that Prussia would stay out of their way. Prussia had a very small navy, and so it had no other option.

Lincoln wanted to declare war against the European powers, but his congress was not so disposed. With the presidential election only four months away, the war in America was enough of an issue without involving more.

In August, General Ulysses S. Grant was paroled and returned to Washington. Although he had given his word not to take up the sword against the Confederacy again, he did give advice. He was convinced that by moving on Richmond and not retreating after a defeat, he could bring the army upon the Confederate capitol and force the issue. Lincoln was a ready convert, but the cabinet knew Grant's track record; he had lost the Armies of the Tennessee and Cumberland by just such a stratagem. Stanton thanked Grant for his advice and then dismissed him. The new strategic situation brought about by the diplomatic defeats required a whole new way of thinking. Congress went home for the summer. The Democrats had nominated George B. McClellan for president.

Joseph E. Johnston now had something like a real army at Meridian. The units he had before were now reorganized, Roddey's cavalry was a separate unit, and the rest were brought together as Lyon's division. It was joined by Loring's division. Johnston had a sufficient force to move northward, at least to Tupelo, but he had conceived another plan, one in which he cooperated with Taylor in a move on New Orleans. He told Davis what he had in mind and was refused on the grounds that communications were impossible as long as the Union controlled the river. Taylor had less ambitious ideas, although he did move down the Red to Alexandria. Davis did not give Johnston an objective, and so he settled on Tupelo. He ran into another move Sturgis was making. Neither was in a defensible position, and so both backed away. At that moment, Forrest turned up. Thus reinforced, Johnston advanced, and Sturgis ran back to Memphis. Johnston recaptured the junction of Corinth, Mississippi, and fortified it. The Union no longer had a railroad from Memphis east. Johnston had communications all the way to New Orleans, but he could not move against it and also defend Corinth. He chose to do the latter, and July passed without another attack.

Richmond was enjoying the large decrease in war attrition. Another brigade was organized at Atlanta to join S. D. Lee, giving him a full-sized division, eight thousand strong. Bragg was now more powerful than Schofield, but he did not want a fight because attrition always aided his enemy. Schofield did not want to fight because he was keeping Bragg away from Nashville as long as his army was intact. Another stalemate.

The Union navy was really cautious now, not wanting to offend the maritime powers. As a result, the blockade was considerably loosened. Food, munitions, and raw materials flowed into the South, cotton flowed out, and European money flowed in. August 1864 brought relief to the Confederate economy. The Europeans always stopped short of any hostile actions, but the situation was perilous. As August marched on, some New Orleans Creoles went to Nassau to talk to the French authorities there. They gave Bazaine complete intelligence of the area and the Union dispositions. The French did not want to be drawn into war, but contingency plans were made for a French amphibious move into Louisiana.

The Union civilian leadership was getting desperate. The military leaders were assuming a completely defensive attitude because none of them wanted to lose a battle. It would be weeks before Congress would assemble again—weeks in which representatives were campaigning. In the Midwestern states, the war was very unpopular. Maryland had wanted to be Confederate from the beginning, but Lincoln had removed its elected legislature by force and installed one that he appointed (also by force). That state had a long memory. Although Union soldiers were stationed everywhere in force, small groups of farmers and villagers began to arm themselves. Southern Ohio was another area where trouble was brewing. This time, even sworn Union soldiers were deserting the cause. They released Confederate prisoners, including John Hunt Morgan, who returned to Tennessee and volunteered to resume the war at Bragg's headquarters. Lincoln slowly realized that he was losing control. No one was volunteering for the army, and there were riots when his agents attempted to enforce the draft. There was order in the country, wherever civilians were in control. Although many young men were in the military, few of them were happy about it. They obeyed orders, but their goal was to be civilians again.

Kentucky had been part of the Union since 1861. The center of resistance was Lexington and was an important rear area for operations in the west. Louisville and Paducah were ports used by the Union navy. There were huge supply stores there. The main Confederate armies were far to the south, but if Schofield ever lost Nashville, Kentucky would be vulnerable. It was divided in sympathy. The Confederate sympathizers would not do anything rash, but they prayed that Bragg would move north.

The Cherokees, who owned slaves, were also sympathetic to the Confederacy. They had actually produced two formed regiments under General Stan Watie, which fought at Pea Ridge. More than two years later, they were once again a threat. This time Watie had about 2,500 men, assembled in what is now eastern Oklahoma. They were ready to move down the Arkansas River to Fort Smith. It only took two weeks before they were threatening the Union position there. After a heavy firefight, they retreated, but not very far. Steele, in Memphis, considered sending Grierson up the Arkansas but decided that he needed him more in front of Corinth.

Lincoln told Meade that he needed a military victory—and that it was up to him. He decided to move toward Fredericksburg, to cross the lower Rappahannock. Lee had another division under D. H. Hill at Raleigh, which he brought up to Cold Harbor to prevent another amphibious wheel like the one McClellan had employed more than two years earlier. Meade prepared pontoon bridges and barges, hoping to get to the lower Rappahannock while Lee was still in the Wilderness position. This was a much less ambitious wheel than McClellan's, which had gone to the end of the peninsula between the York and the James. Meade did get a head start. Lee had a fixed position, except for Stuart's cavalry. The horse soldiers were elected, and they took up a position below Fredericksburg. He got Ewell's men ready to march to the western side of Fredericksburg, but Meade had no intention of crossing there. He simply kept Sedgwick's Corps there to pin Ewell in place. Lee took Longstreet's men east, with A. P. Hill's Corps to follow, and hastened to the heights south of Fredericksburg. Meade had Warren's Corps move toward the bridge, which the local militia burned. The rest of the Army of the Potomac was going farther east, with only Stuart to stop them. That was what Meade thought; he did not know about D. H. Hill. Lee had ordered that formation north from Cold Harbor. Stuart was not alone.

Lee had a hard choice to make. He knew that if he moved Ewell's corps away from the Germanna Ford area, Sedgwick would cross unopposed. He would have to split that force and move part of it to where he had taken his own position. Then he would have to hurry eastward, leaving very little to stop Warren from crossing the bridgeless river at the city. He left Early's division at the ford, and Ed Johnson's at Fredericksburg. Then he hurried to where the crossing was taking place.

But Meade also had a hard choice to make. The roads were narrow. He had to choose between sending the pontoon bridges or sending his artillery. Sheridan's men were leading the way, and they had seven bridges but no guns. They were followed by Burnside, who had artillery, barges, and two bridges. After them came Hancock, who chose to send his artillery first, with his main body following; they had boats but no bridges. As a result, Stuart and Hill had artillery, but Sheridan did not. They did not have enough to cover all the bridges, but they could cover four of them.

The slaughter was dreadful. Sheridan did not give up, because Burnside was right behind him, launching barges and finally setting up artillery to answer the Confederate fire. Burnside's men established a beachhead south of the river—a beachhead that Stuart and Hill did not have the reserves to attack. Around 2:00 p.m., Hancock's artillery arrived and went into action. By then, four of the bridges had been destroyed, but three of Sheridan's and both of Burnside's were still operational. Hancock's infantry was arriving shortly after that with barges and boats. Stuart and Hill retreated toward Spotsylvania Court House. But the battle was not over. Lee arrived with Longstreet's corps and committed them at once. The advance was stalled. A. P. Hill's corps arrived at 4:00 p.m., just as Hancock's main body was crossing. Again the slaughter raged. Meade tried to order Warren to cross in the weakened Confederate front there, but he had no boats to cross the river. The only road was now blocked by the boat transport vehicles, so Warren would not be getting boats. Meade finally went to his last resource: to order Sedgwick to attack Early. Sedgwick did not get the order until sunset and decided to wait until morning.

Sunset found the main attack on the south bank, but all three Union units had taken demoralizing losses. Lee still had Robert Rodes's division, which was fresh and uncommitted. But his cavalry and reserves had retreated and were preparing a defensive position farther south. Sedgwick was ready to attack the Wilderness at dawn, but Early was fortified, and artillery was nearly useless in the woods. Meade chose to move Warren's corps eastward, but the road was terribly clogged. They

FRIED OYSTER SANDWICH

worked their way to the crossing area all night, and by morning they were too tired to move. Hancock's losses were less than Sheridan's or Burnside's, and so he was still combat ready, although just. Both sides had ammunition to spare.

Meade ordered simultaneous attacks by Hancock and Sedgwick in the morning. Sedgwick's failed, but Hancock's made progress. Lee committed Rodes, his last reserve, who forced Hancock to retreat, but by 11:00 a.m., Warren's men were awake and marching. Meade committed them, and Lee ordered the retreat. Sheridan's men were rallying by then, but Burnside's and Hancock's were completely demoralized. Rodes fought as a rearguard so that Lee could make an orderly retreat. Warren's soldiers had had all of three hours' sleep, and they did not press Rodes very hard.

Lee rallied his army at Spotsylvania. The cavalry had already begun fortifications, but they need not have hurried. Meade would not pursue until his Ninth and Second Corps were recovered. Four days later, he made contact with Lee's position and determined it was impregnable. When Lincoln asked him why he wasn't attacking, Meade replied that he would need to replace his losses from Fredericksburg, which would take about sixty days. Neither side had any troops to spare. Meade maintained contact for a week. Another order came from Lincoln to attack. Two days later, a letter came from Halleck relieving Meade of command. He was replaced by General Benjamin Butler, a general who had no respect for Lincoln whatsoever. When Lincoln tried to order Butler to move, he told Lincoln not to interfere with military matters about which he knew nothing. Lincoln tried to remove Butler, but the Massachusetts delegation was furious, calling for impeachment.

Lincoln had one more stratagem. He sent Halleck to command the Army of the Potomac in person. Butler could not talk back to Halleck, who was his military superior. But he could, and did, skulk in his tent like Achilles. The chain of command was interrupted, and the army was stalled. It was just as well. Meade was right about the Confederate position, and Halleck knew it. All Lincoln seemed to care about now was the useless killing of the nation's young men. The generals had more sense.

Fredericksburg was a Union victory, but a Pyrrhic victory. Union losses were three times those of Lee's army. He did take the field from Lee, but the price was far too high. If that were not enough, should they be so foolish as to attack Lee's new position—with interior lines, no woods, and fortifications—the loss ratio would be worse yet. However, Lee also paid a price at Fredericksburg. In the action at the crossing, one of his old, trusted corps commanders, Ambrose Powell Hill, was killed. Lee promoted one of Hill's division commanders, General Richard Anderson. That was the last military action in Virginia.

The French were still interested in the war, but they did not want to fight the Union. They hoped to send Bazaine to Mexico as soon as possible in order to bolster their country's position there. They sent an emissary to New Orleans to try to talk Banks into declaring it an open city. Banks telegraphed Washington and was given a firm negative. Secretary Benjamin was unable to visit his home city because of the occupation. He took the opportunity of visiting it in the company of the French. Because he was their guest, he did not engage in official duties, and so he had nothing to say to Banks, but when the people saw him, they cheered. Popular sentiment in New Orleans was more Confederate than ever. Moreover, the French remembered how Butler had abused New Orleans, which meant that his appointment to the Army of the Potomac appalled them. Though they were irenic in tone, they told Lincoln how greatly the appointment disappointed them. Lincoln was running out of political capital, and so he relieved Butler of command. Massachusetts once again tried to intervene, but they were told that to insist on Butler was to provoke war with France. The Union could not afford that. While England was the only power in the world with a larger navy, the French had two large ironclads that would have brought an end to even the pretense of a blockade. For their part, the French withdrew their request about New Orleans, and the diplomatic situation returned to the *status quo ante*. Secretary Benjamin was aware that the French expected the Confederate States to be active allies against

Juarez. France would give them considerable room as long as they were fighting for their existence, but soon after that, they expected help from the north bank of the Rio Grande. Meanwhile, Taylor moved farther down the Red, setting up a fortified position at Bunkie. He was joined by a company of French-speaking recruits.

September was a calm month. Slocum was no quitter, and he continued trying to attack Charleston from the southeast. Breckinridge had Beauregard's men, which included the garrison, and Stewart's division. He also held three large forts, which were safe from attack. It was not hard to counter Slocum's moves because the latter's choices were very limited. On the tenth, the French fleet made a courtesy call at Charleston. Nobody did anything violent, but the Union navy got out of the way. The blockade was broken in yet another Southern port.

Halleck was perplexed as well. He had conflicting duties as chief of staff and as commander of the Army of the Potomac. He promoted Winfield Scott Hancock to be the commander of the army, placed the Second Corps under Philip Sheridan, and gave the command of the cavalry to John Buford. He completed the promotion by appointing George Armstrong Custer to command the division that had been Buford's. Once he was free to concentrate on his duties as chief of staff, Halleck decided to consolidate the whole army. He left Banks and Steele in place because they were not engaged in any kind of combat, but he recalled Slocum's corps from Charleston and gave it some time off in Annapolis, with the idea of assigning it to the Army of the Potomac. The Confederates paroled all of the prisoners they had taken. Schofield and Banks paroled a large number of Confederate prisoners, and Banks also released all the civilian prisoners held at Fort Massachusetts. Halleck did not chastise them for taking that initiative, so one by one, the Union commanders followed suit. Finally, even Hancock released Lee's men that his army had captured when it was Meade's.

The situation in Ohio was stable. McClellan's campaign headquarters in Cincinnati was very busy. The friction between the army and the citizens had abated; in fact, there was very little left to fight about.

Lincoln knew that his dream of reuniting the nation by force was now beyond realization, and he was becoming reconciled to that notion. Military matters were still his favorite topic of conversation, but in spite of Meade's victory at Fredericksburg, the military was having an unsuccessful year. He wanted Hancock to attack Lee at Spotsylvania, but Halleck refused to order it because the loss of life would be inexcusable. The men in the ranks knew what an attack like that meant, and they were now so reduced in morale that mutiny was a possibility. This was unusual for the Union army, which was the best disciplined fighting force in the world. They were confused at first, expecting the Confederates to attack them. However, the Confederate military leaders knew what a waste that would be; they had no more desire to fight battles than their enemies. There was occasional firing of artillery, especially where Bragg confronted Schofield.

Johnston had a conflict similar to Halleck's. He was commander of the department but also of the army he had assembled. He would yield the latter to Forrest, whose force came to Tupelo to reinforce Johnston's ranks. Steele's lack of activity disappointed Grierson, who wanted to fight to the death. He asked for a transfer, and so Halleck moved him to Nashville. September went as gently as it came. October was the month before the presidential election, and nobody expected Lincoln to win. Davis considered inviting Lincoln to a meeting to discuss ending the conflict while Lincoln was still president. Alexander Stephens disagreed; he had read of Lincoln's negotiating skills and didn't trust Davis to be sufficiently cautious. The Union's congress had reconvened and was badly divided over the war question. The radicals spewed forth venom nobody knew they had, but none of it convinced the realists. Seward's best efforts could not undo England's decision, and the French would no longer talk to him. This was strange because the Union had an army larger than that of the four strongest European powers put together. Even the Confederates were as strong as all but the Prussians and the French. But the Union had had more than three years of fighting for reasons that were not obvious. While the Confederates were defending their homes and farms, women and children, and their slaves, the Union was invading somebody else's ground, destroying property, establishing unpopular occupation governments, and starving women and children with the blockade. At first they were told that force was necessary to preserve the Union. Hundreds of thousands volunteered to do that. But around the beginning of 1863, the war had turned ugly. When the Confederacy suffered reverses, it tried to negotiate an armistice, but the Union civilian and military leaders alike would hear of no other outcome than unconditional surrender. Lincoln held onto that opinion longer than anyone, but as elections approached, he realized that his demand would never happen.

McClellan was elected president of the United States. Lincoln was now a lame duck with limited negotiating powers. The Democrats assembled a rather large majority in both houses of Congress; only New England remained firmly Republican. Lincoln summoned McClellan to Washington, suggesting that they both invite the Confederates to the peace table. Judah Benjamin met with them in a preliminary meeting, and then a second meeting was held in the presence of the French ambassador. Finally, the two presidents, along with Benjamin and Seward, and the new president-elect held a negotiating meeting at Spotsylvania, inside Lee's lines. After five days, they were joined by Hancock and Lee.

Two countries that had fought each other fiercely for four years could hardly be expected to come to a peace agreement in a week. Neither did everybody get the message right away. Taylor's army in Louisiana moved south from Bunkie. They reached the Mississippi at Baton Rouge, at first hiding from the Union gunboats and then wondering why they seemed to ignore them. A young captain from the garrison crossed the river to meet with them, explaining the situation. Banks was sullen and was against peace. He would do whatever Halleck told him, but he would not voluntarily move from New Orleans. Taylor's men and the garrison, both completely armed, lived together in an uneasy ceasefire in Baton Rouge for another week. The Cherokees were another detachment of the South who didn't know of the peace talks. They made one more attempt to take Fort Smith and were repulsed by a division under General Franz Sigel, who had been in St. Louis. The troops in that part of the country were not confident that a truce with the Confederacy also applied to the Cherokee.

As Christmas approached, Varina Davis invited all of the negotiators to Richmond for the celebration. They sent for their families to join them. The talks were suspended in twelve days of fellowship. Secretary Benjamin even led the families in one Chanukah celebration—a little late for any authenticity, but still serving as a welcome adjunct to the Christian festival. Both congresses also had a brief vacation. As Epiphany arrived, the negotiators returned to Spotsylvania. It would now be only two months until McClellan's inauguration, set for the twenty-ninth anniversary of the fall of the Alamo. Little pieces of information kept coming out, but nothing on paper. The two congresses reconvened, and the Confederate congress was in near complete agreement as far as ending the war was concerned. The Union congress was sharply divided over the same question. Still the presidents, secretaries, and generals came to an agreement. They signed it on January 21 with heavy hearts, because that would have been Stonewall Jackson's birthday.

The agreement provided for the following.

1. The Confederate States of America was recognized as a sovereign republic.

2. The eleven states that seceded were joined by Kentucky as a twelfth state in the Confederacy. Maryland and Missouri were retained by the Union. Although there was considerable Confederate sentiment in Maryland, the negotiators did not want to isolate Washington, D.C.

3. The western counties of Virginia were retained by the Union as the state of West Virginia.

4. All remaining prisoners on both sides were unconditionally released.

5. The Union agreed to withdraw its occupying armies as soon as practicable. All offshore forts in the territory of Confederate states were ceded to the Confederacy, with the exception of Fort Jefferson on Dry Tortuga Island.

6. Territories conquered from Mexico west of Texas were retained by the Union.

7. The slave trade was abolished in both republics. States would decide individually concerning the Peculiar Institution itself.

8. Ships from either republic were permitted to call at all ports of the other.

9. Because the Mason-Dixon Line was now completely within the Union, the new border would be the Potomac River, the Ohio River, and the Virginia–West Virginia border in the east, the border between Arkansas and Missouri west of the Mississippi, and the northern and western border of Texas. The Indian Territory was given the option of being part of either republic.

10. Both republics agreed to refrain from aggression against the other.

11. Both republics agreed to a standard railroad gauge. Railroad companies could freely use track in both countries and travel between the two.

12. A rate of exchange was established between the currencies of the two republics.

13. Each republic assumed responsibility for the war and agreed to refrain from requiring reparations from the other.

14. Both agreed that fugitive slaves were to be considered emancipated once in Union territory. This point applied only to fugitives, not to slaves accompanying their masters.

15. Both agreed that there would be no tariffs on trade between the countries.

With these fifteen points of agreement, the negotiators sent the draft to each of the respective congresses. Neither congress was completely happy with the agreement, but in the Confederacy, the approval was almost unanimous. In the Union, the approval was by two-thirds of both houses. Once the agreement was ratified by the legislatures, another committee wrote it up into a treaty, which became known as the Treaty of Spotsylvania.

On March 6, 1865, George B. McClellan was inaugurated as the seventeenth president of the United States. There would be no doubt that the treaty would be honored by all concerned. In August of that year, Robert E. Lee retired from the military. The new Confederate supreme commander would be General James Longstreet.

Jefferson Davis refused a second term as president of the Confederate States. In November 1866, the South elected Richard Taylor as the second president. His father had been president of the United States. Like his father, he intervened in Mexico and helped Maximillian and Carlotta to retain their throne.

Appendix B

The Career of the Confederate Expeditionary Force in the Mexican War

THE CONFEDERATE STATES HAD AN obligation to France because of the latter's help in lifting the blockade and giving them diplomatic recognition. As soon as the Treaty of Spotsylvania was signed, they began to organize a means to help the French representative in Mexico, Emperor Maximillian von Habsburg, and his consort, Carlotta von Saxe-Coburg. Though the temptation to demobilize was strong, the debt to France was a matter of honor.

Robert E. Lee decided he was finished with all things military. After receiving honors for his command of the Army of Northern Virginia, he retired to this estate at Arlington. James Longstreet became the chairman of the military and naval departments. President Davis appointed General Pierre G. T. Beauregard as chief of staff for military operations. He allowed a partial demobilization, but a standing army remained in the field. Robert Rodes's division was sent to New Orleans, Wade Hampton's cavalry went to Pensacola, and a large force began to assemble at Brownsville, Texas, on the Rio Grande, under the command of Major General Richard Ewell, who was named commander in chief of the Confederate Expeditionary Force. This was divided into three divisions, the first under General John Bell Hood, the second under General John Pender, and the third under General William Loring. In addition to these, there were 5,000 cavalry under General John Hunt Morgan, and about 1,600 Cherokee volunteers under General Stan Watie.

On April 11, 1865, there was a massacre of three hundred Belgian troops by the Juaristas at Tacámbaro. In response to that, the Confederate congress declared war against the Juaristas. Beauregard at once sent Rodes and Hampton to Veracruz, and Ewell crossed the Rio Grande and occupied Matamoros. Watie took his volunteers to Laredo and crossed the Rio Grande there.

The Juaristas had the imperial army outnumbered. They held Querétaro to the north, Puebla to the east, and all that was south of Villahermosa. The previous summer, Bazaine's French corps had defeated a Juarista army under Porfirio Diaz at Oaxaca, which kept the southern portion of the Juarista army away from the capitol. The imperial army was divided between the commands of Leonardo Marquez and Miguel Miramon, mainly deployed against Juarez's main body to the north, with Bazaine, who had been reinforced by six thousand Austrians under General Franz Thun were between the capital and Puebla. The Belgian cavalry, after the loss of its detachment at Tacámbaro, numbered about nine hundred and served as a reserve in Chapúltepec.

As soon as he had Matamoros secured, Ewell marched on Monterey. Juarez now had a dilemma: either make more detachments or leave one or more fronts unguarded. He sent seven thousand men to try to secure Monterey, but Ewell arrived first with superior numbers. He had time to prepare a defensive position south of the city. When the Juarista detachment arrived, it attacked and was routed. Juarez took his main body to Puebla to cut communications between Veracruz and Chapúltepec. Within a week, Rodes was marching toward Puebla, and when they discovered that French marines were enough to hold Veracruz, which had pro-imperial city officials, Hampton soon followed. Juarez was caught between Bazaine on the west and Rodes and Hampton on the east. Meanwhile, Watie moved on Saltillo, which after the battle at Monterey had only poorly trained guerillas to offer resistance. Watie's Cherokees easily brushed these aside.

The Confederates' superior artillery and small arms took a toll on the Mexicans whenever they clashed. Even though Juarez outnumbered the combined French and Confederate armies he was facing, his losses were triple those of his enemies. His one great advantage was that Bazaine was not in communication with Rodes and Hampton, but both crafty generals knew whether or not there was resistance in front of them; if there was none, they marched toward Puebla. Soon Juarez would be surrounded. Rather than let that happen, he withdrew his main body to Querétaro.

Ewell wanted to establish a seaborne supply line as he moved south, and so he sent Hood's division to secure the port of Tampico. Some two thousand Texas militia were sent to occupy Monterey as the Expeditionary Force moved toward San Luis Potosi. Watie approached the same objective. Rodes and Hampton made contact with Bazaine at Puebla, where they halted to regroup.

At this point the imperial, Confederate, and French forces were able to meet and plan a coordinated offensive. Marquez's division was sent south to counterattack any Juarista move from Oaxaca. Miramon, Lopez's lancers, and the Belgians would move northward slowly but remained in quick return distance from the capital. Bazaine would move toward Pachuco, where he would assemble with Rodes and Hampton. As for Ewell, he waited until Hood's division was back with the main group, and then he moved quickly against San Luis Potosi.

Juarez realized that sending any more detachments was suicide; his best hope now was to fight a slow retreat of attrition. There were some forces loyal to him in the south, but he was not in contact with them. If the allies made detachments, he could pick them off. That did not happen. They concentrated in two huge forces, Ewell's and Bazaine's. Once Ewell arrived at San Luis Potosi and Bazaine arrived at Pachuco, they stopped. Juarez had more than either of them, but less than both.

Miramon was a third allied force that was only about 8,500 men. But Juarez could not afford to go after it, or else he could be attacked on the flank by Bazaine and from the rear by Ewell.

The allies did not need to attack. Juarez did not have sources of supply for his main body. The allies had the capital and the ports of Veracruz and Tampico. They controlled all of northern and central Mexico. Juarez had no allies. The United States had been his ally, but after McClellan was elected president, the Republicans were out of favor. The Democrats didn't want any more bloodshed, so Juarez was on his own.

He waited at Querétaro for the allies to move. They didn't. July and August passed, but the situation did not change. The north was being pacified. Juarez sent a detachment to Celaya to try to establish a supply line from the west. Miramon went after it, and there was a brief battle, which the Juaristas won. But now Bazaine and Ewell knew the detachment had been made, and they both moved toward Querétaro. Miramon retreated toward the capital. Juarez tried to recall the detachment, but they wanted to pursue Miramon. They ran out of supplies trying to catch him. Juarez decided to abandon Querétaro, but it was too late. Ewell was a few miles north of it. His Whitworth guns were in range of it. Two days later, Bazaine arrived, and the siege was complete.

Juarez asked for a truce. Ewell sent word to Maximillian, and the emperor came to Querétaro to personally conduct the parlay. Matters did not take long. Juarez knew his position was hopeless. Bazaine asked the US ambassador to grant Juarez asylum in San Francisco. This was granted. His army surrendered and was paroled. Diaz was a prisoner in the capital, but he was released to join Juarez in exile. Except for isolated pockets in the south, the war was over.

The Confederate Expeditionary Force moved to Chapúltepec, where all its parts were assembled and reorganized. They moved to Oaxaca and then headed eastward to Yucatan, wiping out all the pockets of resistance and organizing local pro-imperial militias. It took until the new year before all was pacified, but 1866 proved to be the birth of a great Mexican nation. Beauregard came to Veracruz personally to make the awards. On the twenty-first, the anniversary of the birth of Stonewall Jackson, the Confederate Expeditionary Force was disbanded; the units were transported to New Orleans and Pensacola to be mustered out. Ewell remained in Mexico for the rest of his life. He had become very close in friendship to General Félix Douay, Bazaine's second in command. He was given a pension and rooms at Chapúltepec, and he became part of the retinue of the Empress Carlotta. Bazaine and Douay returned to France, where they suffered a humiliating defeat four years later at the hands of the Prussians.

Appendix C

Presidents of the Confederate States of America

Jefferson Davis ---- Mississippi ----- 1861–1866
Richard Taylor ---- Louisiana ------ 1867–1872
Alexander Stephens ----- Georgia ----- 1873–1878
John C. Breckinridge—South Carolina – 1879–1884
Simon B. Buckner --- Kentucky ---------- 1885–1890
Wade Hampton ----- South Carolina -- 1891–1896
Francis T. Nicholls --- Louisiana ------- 1897–1902

Joseph Wheeler ---- Alabama ---------- 1903–1908
Joseph Draper Sayers --- Texas -------- 1909–1920
In 1920, the constitution was amended to limit the term of office to four years, but permitting a second term.
Austin Peay ----------- Tennessee -------- 1921–1927 (died in office)
Joseph Ransdell ---- Louisiana ---------- 1927–1928
Harry F. Byrd --- Virginia --------------1929–1936
John Hollis Bankhead II --- Alabama --- 1937–1940

J. Strom Thurmond ---- South Carolina -- 1941–1948
Albert Benjamin Chandler --- Kentucky -- 1949–1952
W. Kerr Scott ----- North Carolina ------- 1953–1956
James Oliver Eastland ----- Mississippi --- 1957–1964
Buford Ellington ---- Tennessee ----------- 1965–1968

Samuel Ervin ----- North Carolina -------- 1969–1976
David H. Pryor --- Arkansas -------------- 1977–1980

CPSIA information can be obtained
at www.ICGtesting.com
Printed in the USA
FFOW04n1418100617
36597FF

9 781524 688721